BORN
in the YEAR of
COURAGE

BORN
in the YEAR *of*
COURAGE

by Emily Crofford

Carolrhoda Books, Inc./Minneapolis

This book is available in two editions:
Library binding by Carolrhoda Books, Inc.
Soft cover by First Avenue Editions
Divisions of Lerner Publishing Group
241 First Avenue North
Minneapolis, MN 55401 U.S.A.

Website address: www.lernerbooks.com

LIBRARY OF CONGRESS CATALOGING-IN-PUBLICATION DATA

Crofford, Emily.
    Born in the year of courage / by Emily Crofford
        p.   cm. (Adventures in Time)
    Summary: In 1841, having been shipwrecked and picked up
by an American whaling ship outside Japanese territorial waters,
fifteen-year-old Manjiro decides to go live in America and work
towards opening trade between his country and the West.
    ISBN: 0-87614-679-5 (lib. bdg.)
    ISBN: 1-57505-424-8 (pbk.)
    1. Nakahama, Manjiro, 1827–1898—Juvenile fiction.
[1. Nakahama, Manjiro, 1827–1898—fiction. 2. Japan—History—
1787–1868—Fiction. 3. Shipwrecks—Fiction. 4. Whaling—Fiction.]
I. Title.
PZ7.C873Bo 1991
[Fic]—dc20   91-10883

Manufactured in the United States of America
    6 7 8 - BP - 05 04

To Samantha Faith Bordages

Author's Note

When my father died, many years after Mother's death, we children found an official paper from the U. S. Navy in their old steamer trunk. Daddy had told stories about his years at sea; he had not told us he received the Navy Cross for "extraordinary heroism" during World War I. And the family records in his Bible revealed that one of his brothers, his father, and his grandfather were named for Oliver Hazard Perry. What, I wondered, was Daddy's connection to this naval hero of the War of 1812?

I didn't find it when I read about Oliver Hazard Perry, but the books led me to read about his brother, Commodore Matthew Calbraith Perry. Some of those books included brief references to Manjiro. I wanted to know more, but tracking down Manjiro's story was not easy. He never sought glory. He acted with courage because he cared about others.

Sometimes it takes a while to make the right connection.

Some years ago I read a small article about Manjiro. It would not leave my mind, and in time he moved into the house and stood at my elbow while I wrote his story. Occasionally he was uncertain about last names. If any are wrong, we apologize to descendants.

Manjiro's descendants, some of whom live in the United States and Canada, believe as he did—that oceans link rather than separate.

For their generous help, I am particularly indebted to Yoshi Yabuuchi Williams, a native of Kyoto, Honshu; Alice Sanoden, who lived for thirty-six years in Japan; my son Bob, student of history and world religions; and Pat Gerlach, librarian.

Introduction

P resent-day Japan is known for its democratic system and trade relations with countries throughout the world. It was a very different land when Manjiro, a commoner born in 1827, lived there in his youth.

Commoners like Manjiro were not allowed a family name. They had to bow when a feudal lord, a *daimyo*, approached. The lord had complete power over his people, who were essentially slaves. It was known that if the bow was not made quickly enough, and the *daimyo* was in a dark mood, he might tell one of his knights, the samurai who attended him, to cut off the offender's head.

This was part of a military-civil system that began in the twelfth century when the emperor's general, or shogun, won control of all of Japan's islands. The emperor, as the descendant of the sun god and goddess who created the islands, was still considered the divine ruler. But from the twelfth century forward, his chief duty was to confer titles.

As the years passed, some shoguns were assassinated. Others were incompetent. Without central rule, lords fought other lords for land and power. Soon, Japan had hundreds of rulers and constant war. Corruption, thievery, and murder were everywhere.

The centuries of turmoil affected the mental and emotional balance of the people, who believed in order, and that the welfare of the group was more important than that of the individual.

Shogun Hideyoshi, who came into power in 1582, established the order the people craved when he restored national unity. Hideyoshi grouped the people into four classes: samurai, farmer, artisan, and merchant. The samurai, from the shogun down to lowest-ranking warriors, were the ruling class. The other three classes, the commoners, were heavily taxed to support the samurai but had no voice in even the lowest level of government. There was also a fifth group, *etta*, the untouchables who handled corpses and animal carcasses. *Etta* were not considered a class; they were treated as if they were invisible.

Hideyoshi believed trade would benefit Japan. He traded with Europe, Siam, China, Korea, and other countries. He allowed Portuguese and then Spanish missionaries to come to his country because he thought that would influence Spain and Portugal to trade more with Japan.

But in 1592, Hideyoshi decided to first take over Korea, then to conquer China, which of course halted trade with those countries. He also turned against the missionaries. They were inclined to be arrogant, and he realized that they were not going to help bring about trade. They only wanted to convert people to Christianity.

The war finally ended in 1598 when Hideyoshi died. He left no suitable heir, and a few years later, a man named Ieyasu seized power and founded the Tokugawa Shogunate.

Ieyasu distrusted the missionaries even more than Hideyoshi had. He became convinced that their Christianizing was part of a plan to conquer Japan. Spain and Portugal, he thought, were vanguards of the Western Imperialists—the barbarians, the feet that trampled. (The Japanese scholars' map of the world was like a chart of the human body with Japan at the top—the head. Europe and America were the legs and feet.)

By the time Ieyasu died in 1616, suspicion of the missionaries' intent had grown strong. They were branded southern barbarians and ordered to leave—the Spanish in the Exclusion Edict of 1624, the Portuguese in 1638. Many did not leave and were executed. Japanese Christians were persecuted, and when they rebelled, almost forty thousand were massacred.

The 1638 edict also stated that any Japanese who left the country could return only under penalty of death.

The only foreigners allowed to stay in Japan were the Dutch, who had come in the early 1600s and never tried to convert anyone. As representatives of the Dutch East India Company, their only interest was in trade. They served as Japan's eyes to the West. But they were restricted to the tiny island of Deshima, and only one Dutch ship could come each year.

Japan was again carrying on a little trade with China, but ships from all other nations were forbidden to enter ports at any of the many Japanese or Japanese-controlled islands. Restrictions within the country were just as severe. Commoners had to account for their whereabouts twenty-four hours a day.

Eventually there was no need to remind them of the old edict stating that if they left Japan they would face death if they returned. Manjiro, a fisherman's son who lived in the village of Nakanohama, on the island of Shikoku, did not know the law existed.

1
The Storm

anjiro lay wondering why he had awakened with a sense of foreboding. This new year was the Year of the Cow (1841 in the Western calendar)—a lucky year.

It must be, he decided, that the secret fear that he would fail his family had made itself into a forgotten bad dream. He had told no one that being registered as head of the household concerned him. That would soon happen now that he was fifteen. He had been the main provider for his mother, his brother, and his three sisters since his father's death five years ago, but that was different from being *registered*. Everyone in Nakanohama would be watching to see if he lived up to the honor.

He would have to guard against having notions about better ways to do things. If he had new ideas or did something in a way that was different from the way it had always been done, he would cause scandal for himself and his family. Only recently a villager had hired him to polish rice, and to make the job go faster, Manjiro had mixed pebbles in the mortar. It had worked well, but the man had been upset. He had come to Manjiro's house and said to his mother, "No one has ever mixed pebbles in the mortar!"

His eyes still closed, Manjiro whispered, "I will not have any more ideas. I will be a worthy head of household."

When he opened his eyes, he saw that the sun was also awakening. Its glow through the oilpaper windows made paths across the *goza*, the straw mats that insulated Manjiro and his family from the cold, damp earth floor. He pulled himself to a sitting position. His mother and two of his sisters were already up, moving around in the *daidokoro* as they prepared the morning meal. His brother and his little sister were stirring.

Manjiro's spirits lifted. Today was indeed a lucky day. Fudenojo, a respected fisherman who lived in Nishihama Usaura, a short distance away, had invited

Manjiro to work with his crew. And the sea bass would be running, as they always did with the coming of the New Year. He would share in the profits from the sale of the fish they caught. He could buy charcoal for cooking, and rice, and other supplies his family badly needed.

He had taken a hot bath last evening, so now he quickly dressed in the clothing fishermen wore: short kimono, *shigoki* (a narrow cloth belt), *momohiki* (knee pants), and *waragi* (straw sandals). Before combing his hair and arranging it the way he liked it, with a narrow cloth tie at the back, Manjiro glanced around to be sure his sisters weren't watching. They teased that he was vain, and he knew there was truth in their teasing. He was proud of his fine hair, his nicely shaped head, his chiseled face and wide mouth with a full bottom lip. He didn't look like a peasant, he sometimes told himself. He looked like a young lord.

When he and the rest of his family had eaten, he was impatient to leave, to be away from his mother's unspoken worry. *"Ittekimasu, Okaasan,"* he said. (I will go and come back, Mother.)

He saw a reminder in her face that he had neglected to do something. He knew what he had not done, but after all, he would only be gone a few days. He hurried away, and as he left Nakanohama behind him, his spirits soared even higher. It was a wonderful day, a day for walking—a day for fishing.

But as he neared Usaura, a nagging regret began to

hang like a cloud in his mind. He should have gone to the village burial grounds and reported to his father that he was leaving on a fishing trip. It had upset his mother that he had not done so.

But he could not take the time to go back. Many things had to be done to prepare for fishing. If he didn't do his share, Fudenojo might not ask him again. Word would spread, and he would surely not be able to provide well for his family. He walked on.

It was said that inland on his island of Shikoku, it was cold in January. But here the breeze blew warm off the Pacific Ocean. Savoring the exciting smell of fish and salt water, Manjiro looked up and down the rocky shore at the men checking their sails and readying their boats for fishing. When he spotted Fudenojo, a lean, thin-faced man of thirty-eight, and the rest of the crew he would work with, he called greetings: *"Ohayo go zai masu!"*

Fudenojo nodded to acknowledge Manjiro's arrival, and his gentle-faced brother Juusuke, who was in his late twenties, smiled. Fudenojo's friend Toraemon, the most muscular of the group, did not look up from whatever task he was bent over.

Fudenojo and Juusuke's stocky brother Goemon, who was only a little older than Manjiro, called and waved. Goemon was quite spoiled, and Manjiro thought his brothers were as responsible for his spoiling as their mother. He liked Goemon, though, and was glad of the company of someone only a year older than he.

His and Goemon's job was to empty the nets. But if the older men brought in many fish, Manjiro thought, they would surely let Goemon and him take a turn with the nets.

"This will be a lucky day," Manjiro said when he reached the others.

"Yes," Goemon said. "I don't know why we must take so many supplies. We'll have a full catch before day's end. We could replenish our supplies before we go out again tomorrow."

"It may be a lucky day for the fish," Fudenojo said dryly. "That is why we prepare to stay out for three days."

Manjiro and the others waded back and forth carrying water, charcoal and kindling, rice and bait out to the twenty-four-foot fishing boat. Up and down the shore, other fishermen were doing the same.

The other fishing boats looked very much like Fudenojo's. The sterns were "open"—squared off and flat on a level with the sides of the boat. The boats would easily swamp in open sea. Manjiro knew the design was for the fishermen's own welfare. If a boat was seaworthy, it might venture out too far.

As if his thoughts followed Manjiro's, Goemon said, "This is a sturdy boat, and it is in good repair. We could fish beyond the waters we know."

"Do not say such things," Fudenojo said a little sharply. "We must never even think about fishing in waters contaminated by barbarians."

Manjiro shuddered. The barbarians must be terrifying to behold. The wise old man in Manjiro's village claimed to have seen some in his youth when their leaking ship came into a port at another of Dai Nippon's islands. He didn't explain how he had happened to be on another island when one had to have papers even to visit another province. But Manjiro didn't doubt the truth of the wise man's story. He had described in detail what the barbarians who lived at the feet of the world looked like. They had big noses, hairy faces—and *blue* eyes.

The fishermen ate their lunch of pickled turnips, rice, and tea. Fudenojo made one last check; Manjiro and the others climbed into the boat.

Hours later, when the sun had slid low, Goemon motioned toward a boat within view that was heading for shore. "It has been a good day for some," he said, "but not for us."

Their catch was indeed meager, Manjiro thought. Surely tomorrow would be better.

Fudenojo steered the boat behind a rock to shelter them from the wind. The waves rocked the boat gently; the soft splashes were like a lullaby. Manjiro didn't want to miss anything, but he couldn't stay awake to listen to the older men's stories.

The second night came and still they had only a few fish. Again Fudenojo sought shelter behind a rock. They ate and talked, then slept.

Late the next day, Juusuke said, "Look!"

Manjiro drew in his breath. The water was alive with fish!

Mackerel and sea bream ran in schools so large that Toraemon threw out five buckets of nets. By the time Manjiro and Goemon emptied one net, the other men were bringing in another. Manjiro vaguely noticed that clouds were building, but he was too pleased with their catch to be concerned about clouds.

The sky darkened; a twisting wind began to blow.

"We must pull in our nets and head for shore," Fudenojo said.

Even while Manjiro and Toraemon hauled in the nets, the storm became more intense. The sky and the sea turned black. The wind shrieked. Freezing rain came down in streams. Juusuke struggled to wrap the sail around the mast. He had no sooner done so when the mast broke.

Fudenojo, in the open forward space, at the tiller connected to the rudder, cried out that he had no control. Manjiro saw that the peg that held the rudder oar had broken. An instant later, the oar itself broke in two.

They tried to row and guide the boat with the oars fishermen always took with them. The sea snatched the oars away.

To keep from screaming, Manjiro prayed as the wrecked boat, now like a piece of flotsam, rode up and up to the top of a wave, plunged down into the trough, and rose again.

2
A Rock Island

The wind howled. Cold rain came in slanting sheets. The sea raged. Over and over Manjiro and the others said, *"Namuamidabutsu."* (I believe in Buddha.)

At last the storm subsided and the sea calmed.

When morning came, Manjiro could see nothing of Shikoku or the other islands except for the mountains. In the day's sun, their clothing dried, but the night stretched long and cold.

With the coming of dawn on the second day, Manjiro

watched the tops of the tallest mountains disappear. "There is only water now," Goemon said. "And it has changed color. It is much darker."

Goemon was right, Manjiro realized. Not only that, but the boat kept to a path, as if it were being pulled along by some invisible creature.

Fudenojo rubbed his hand over his face. "We are caught in Kuroshio, the Black Current, which runs like a river through the sea."

Even if they had not been caught in an ocean river, Manjiro thought, they would be helpless.

They still had their flint and steel, but they could not make fire because the faggots and charcoal were soaked through. Their remaining rice had been drenched with seawater. Fudenojo had thrown it overboard. They would not go hungry, though. They had plenty of fish to eat.

After sunset that day, the spray was so cold that Manjiro shook violently. He put his hand to his hair and realized that icicles hung in it. A thin sheet of ice spread over his kimono.

The boat moved steadily forward, and the view was always the same: waves broad at the bottom, curling over at the top in a sea that seemed to touch the sky on every side of them. If not for the marks Fudenojo made with a knife on the broken mast, Manjiro thought dully, he would not know that five days had passed since the storm.

It had sleeted once, and they had caught the sleet in their buckets. Another time it had rained, but not for very long. Although they had drunk seldom and sparingly, the water they caught was soon gone. Manjiro thought it had been two days ago when they put the last drops on their tongues. They still had two nets and had brought in fresh fish. Fudenojo said that even a fish that lived in salt water had a little fresh water in its flesh. He must stop thinking about water! Doing so increased his thirst.

"Birds," Goemon murmured.

Manjiro lifted his head. Goemon was right. Ahead of them, birds wheeled. Albatross! Circling and settling albatross meant land!

Through the night, he dozed and jerked awake, and dozed again. Each time he awakened, he said in his mind, Rise, oh sun, bring light. Show us the land where the birds roost. What if they passed the land during the night? What if they saw it with the coming of morning, but the current did not take them to it?

At last dawn came. They were headed directly toward a small island. Rock! The island was not land. It was made of rock. At one end, the rocks reached high, like craggy hills. After a low point in the middle of the island, the rocks rose again, but not nearly so high as they did at the other end. The swift current was taking them directly toward the island. When the boat hit those rocks, it would splinter!

Even as Fudenojo said, "We must leave the boat!" Manjiro jumped into the sea.

When it closed over his head, he thought for a moment that the very cold would crush him. But he quickly surfaced and saw that Toraemon and Goemon were also swimming.

Where were Fudenojo and Juusuke? They must still be in the boat. But where was it? There it was, upside down. Fudenojo and Juusuke must be trapped underneath it!

In the next instant the boat seemed to explode. Fudenojo and Juusuke were free; they were swimming.

Manjiro reached the island, climbed upward to dry rock, and lay on his stomach gasping for breath. When he could sit up, he saw Fudenojo and Juusuke walking toward him and the others.

Fudenojo sank down beside Toraemon. "The boat hit an underwater rock," he said.

All of them had bruises, and Juusuke and Fudenojo were bleeding from scrapes, but only Juusuke seemed to be really hurt. He was pale and in obvious pain.

"My foot is injured," Juusuke said.

Fudenojo examined his brother's foot. "It is badly bruised," he said. "A small bone may be broken."

Manjiro stood up, but when he took a step, the motion of the sea was still so strong in him that he fell. He got to his feet, leaned against a rock for a moment, then set out again. He still staggered, but this time he did not fall.

Water. He had to find water for them. In a hollow of a rock, like a shallow bowl, he found fresh rainwater. *"Mizu,"* he called through his parched lips.

It took all his will, but he waited until the others joined him, and they bowed their heads and put their hands together in a prayer of thanksgiving. Then one by one, Juusuke first because he was hurt, they scooped water up in trembling hands and drank.

Manjiro lay down on the warm stone then and felt himself slipping into sleep. The same thing, he realized vaguely, was happening to the others.

When he awoke, the sun and the strong breeze had dried his clothes. Looking around, he felt hopeful. The island, which he estimated at two miles around, was inhabited, if only by birds. Albatross stood on nearby rocks. While his friends came up from their sleep, he rose to his feet, walked a little away from them, and looked around. Surely plants grew somewhere on the island. He just couldn't see them.

"Now we must find food," Goemon said. "Something besides fish."

"Albatross?" Manjiro asked, and was pleased when the others laughed with him.

An albatross lit on an outcrop of rock almost within arm's reach and gazed at Manjiro. His laughter died. They could salvage other things from their wrecked boat, but their flint and steel had surely sunk; they could not make fire, even though the reeds growing along the water line would serve as fuel. What if they found no edible plants here? Eating a good fish's delicate, almost bloodless flesh raw was one thing, but eating raw albatross, which didn't hesitate to dine on entrails and other refuse, was quite another.

At least they were safe. Would his mother somehow know? He pictured himself walking into their house, saw her coming to embrace him when they were rescued and he went home. Fishing boats from Shikoku could not come this far to search for them, but surely fishermen from one of Dai Nippon's other islands would come.

Or maybe a Dutch ship would rescue them. The wise man said that Dutch ships came to Deshima. He could tie his kimono to a piece of their boat . . .

Stop, Manjiro told himself sternly. He must not ponder and anticipate and try to think what to do. More than once, he had heard elders counsel, "If you are troubled and try to think what to do, your opponent will surely strike you down."

But who was the opponent here? They were friends, brothers to each other.

The answer to his question came so swiftly Manjiro could not stop it: death is the opponent.

He shook his head sharply to dislodge the thought so he could understand what Fudenojo was saying.

"Juusuke, sit here in the sun," Fudenojo said. "The rest of us will look for shelter and food."

His gentle face serene now that he had adjusted to the pain of his injured foot, Juusuke nodded.

If the four of them split into pairs, Manjiro thought as they left Juusuke, they could cover the island more quickly. He waited to see if Fudenojo would make the suggestion. When he didn't, Manjiro said, "If two of us went one way, and two another..."

Fudenojo looked at him, and for a split second Manjiro saw resentment in his eyes. "We will stay together," Fudenojo said.

Manjiro looked away. He would have to remember that here he was not the head of a family, that Fudenojo was the leader.

They found more water in rock hollows and drank again—and again. What if they were not rescued for many days? Manjiro wondered. Or weeks. Would there be enough rain to fill the hollows they were draining dry? He said nothing. He did not look at Fudenojo, lest the older man see the question in his face.

When they found green shoots growing in a crack, they squatted and studied them. "I think they are shoots of the *kaya* tree," Toraemon said. "But here they can never become trees." He broke off a piece of a shoot, smelled it, and tasted it. "At any rate, they are not poisonous."

Manjiro and the others put their palms together, bowed their heads, and said, *"Itadakimasu."* (I am going to eat.)

After eating some of the shoots, they oriented themselves so they could find the plants on the way back and take some to Juusuke.

"Today we will not try to scale the high end of the island," Fudenojo said. "We'll explore the other end—which I think faces the sea-lanes for ships. As we go, we will search for shelter."

Manjiro studied the rock formations as they climbed but saw nothing that would offer shelter. When they were near the edge of the rocks, Manjiro stopped walking and felt as if he were going to be sick. The stones in two body-length mounds had obviously been placed there by human hands—and wooden markers were anchored in one end of each mound.

"It looks as if someone carved or scratched their names," Fudenojo said.

Toraemon shook his head. "Who could know whether they were from one of our islands or from some barbarian land? The rain and wind have erased the letters."

Not far from the graves, Goemon found a skeleton.

Manjiro swallowed. There had been no one left to cover that one with stones.

On the way back to Juusuke, an albatross alit on Manjiro's shoulder. He did not stop to ponder what to do. As if by reflex, he swiftly reached up and grabbed the albatross by one of its legs. While it struggled to free itself, he closed his other hand around its neck.

3

Learning to Survive

Manjiro watched Fudenojo, who was growing a chin beard, make another mark on a piece of driftwood. They had been on the island for four days now, and they still had not found shelter.

Shaking from the cold, Manjiro knew he would never again take fire for granted. Toraemon gathered reeds, wove them together, and pounded them to make them thin as paper. He then laid them on a stone and struck them again and again with another stone. Sometimes sparks would fly, but he could not make fire.

Manjiro told himself to think about the good things that had happened. Boards from the wrecked boat had washed ashore along with two buckets and a piece of canvas. They had torn off a strip of the canvas to make a signal flag, and Toraemon had placed the buckets at the bottom of a slanting rock to catch the runoff when it rained.

"We will not drink from the buckets unless we have to," Fudenojo had said. "They are our wells." He dubbed one of the buckets *Ido*, Well of Springwater, and the other *Izumi*, Well of Life.

"We have much to be grateful for," Manjiro whispered to himself.

The next morning, relishing the feel of the sun-warmed rock on the bottoms of his bare feet, he went with Goemon to explore part of the island they had not carefully covered before. From the morning they had found the island, the rocks had intrigued him. They were of various shapes and sizes, and the formations were especially interesting. Some were as graceful as an artist's drawing; others were jumbled stacks.

Violent storms, Manjiro thought, had probably caused some of the big rocks near the tops of the rock hills to fall to a lower ledge and break into pieces. Over time, wind and rain had smoothed and rounded the smaller stones, then another storm had sent them sliding down like a waterfall.

There, for instance, stood a mound of small rocks in

front of big slabs. The heap of small rocks was deeper and wider at the bottom than at the top. Manjiro kept looking at the mound. It was different from any other formation he had seen on the island.

He picked up one of the rocks from near the top of the pile. The one behind it fell inward.

He stared at Goemon; Goemon looked back at him with wide eyes. They grabbed rocks, threw them aside, and peered into blackness.

"A cave," Manjiro whispered.

He and Goemon hugged each other and danced a circle, chanting, then shouting as they ran back to the others, "A cave, a cave, we have found a cave!"

The cave was large enough for all of them, with room to spare. It was clammy inside, and their own breath made it damper still. But it would shelter them from storms and from the cold night wind.

"There is no sign that the other poor castaways ever slept here," Fudenojo said.

"If it hadn't been for Manjiro, we might never have found it," Goemon said. "You know how fascinated he is with the rocks."

Manjiro gave a small smile. It was all very puzzling. When he had pondered how he could make the rice polishing faster, it had led to getting into trouble. But as Goemon had just said, if he had not kept wondering about the rocks, they might never have found the cave.

"The wood from our boat will serve as beds," Fudenojo

said. "And a piece of the canvas will be our door."

Finding the cave was a good sign that their luck was changing, Manjiro thought. He was full of hope when he took his turn the next day and went to the lookout point where they had placed their signal flag.

As he sat down, he was aware of the nearby graves. There were three mounds of stones now. Fudenojo and Toraemon had covered the skeleton.

Those three also watched, but a ship never came for them—a thought, so strong it was like spoken words, came into Manjiro's mind. He rubbed his fingers across his forehead to erase the thought. Those others had probably been injured or sick when they arrived here.

Through the following weeks, he said many times, "This is a promising day. This is the day a ship will pass our way."

One day Goemon came running to say that there was a ship, but when the others went to the lookout spot, they saw nothing.

After a silent morning meal of raw albatross eggs, Manjiro walked to the shore and looked out at the waves. They were dark blue at the bottom, white at the crest. And their ceaseless slapping against the rocks could become hypnotizing. One could understand how Goemon thought he saw a ship.

Thinking about Goemon running toward them, his arms pumping, his hair flying while he shouted, "A ship! A ship!" made laughter bubble up in Manjiro.

He went back to the others, put his hands over his eyes, and looking into space, shouted, "A ship! A ship is coming."

Even Goemon laughed.

As the day wore on, Manjiro, Toraemon, and Juusuke repeated the performance, until Fudenojo moved his hand in a gesture that indicated, "Enough. No more teasing."

Manjiro faced Goemon and lowered his eyes long enough to indicate apology, but not so long that Goemon would feel compelled to reply by word or sign that the teasing hadn't bothered him. That would be an untruth, and Manjiro would be responsible for the untruth.

They had learned that the albatross tasted better if they pounded it with a rock and let it dry on warm stone. They found other food, too. Wading around the island, they gathered shellfish. For a vegetable in their diet, they ate seaweed that washed up on the rocks at the waterline. But the shellfish and seaweed increased thirst. Rains had been scanty; the hollows held only a little water now.

Each day they removed their clothing and bathed in the sea. On occasion they washed their clothes. Manjiro found a small, rough-edged stone and rubbed it against his fingernails and toenails to keep them from growing so long. He had lost his hair tie when he swam from the boat to the island, and he did not want to tear off a piece of his *obi* to make a tie as Toraemon had done, so he plaited green reeds to hold his hair in place. Thinking of how his sisters would tease him about being vain even on a deserted rock island, he smiled.

In the next instant, tears ran down his cheeks, and his insides ached with homesickness.

By the end of the second month, the albatross no longer alit on their shoulders or even came close. The birds perched at the top of the high, steep rock formations.

"They know they're safe there," Juusuke said with a thin smile.

"They only think they're safe," Manjiro said. "Have you not seen me practicing?"

"I've seen you throwing stones," Juusuke said.

"You'll never be able to hit one," Goemon said.

Manjiro continued to practice, and a day came when he decided he was ready. He scarcely believed it himself when he threw the stone and an albatross fell from its high perch and hit the rock below with a thud.

With more practice, he became such an expert that the others teased him when he *missed*.

The third month passed. The albatross chicks learned to fly, and the colony left.

"Surely they will come back," Goemon said.

"When their migration brings them back to nest,"

Fudenojo said. "That will be many months from now."

"By that time they will not need to fear us," Juusuke said. "We will be dead."

"Since the day we were caught in the storm, we have had many signs that we are cared for," Manjiro said. "We will not die. We are going to be rescued."

As the days grew warmer, and the winter rains stopped, his hope waned. They had to drink from the buckets now, and even though Fudenojo had cut their ration to one small shellful a day, the water level went down quickly. The thirst was always there, their mouths so dry they could not even produce saliva to ease the body's plea for water.

Manjiro smiled ruefully when he remembered that he had once written a poem about the beauty of the stars. Now, if a small cloud appeared at night when he was outside the cave, he found himself saying, "Cover them, clouds! Cover the stars!"

Juusuke spent more and more time in the cave. "Fireflies," he whispered late one afternoon when he was in the cave and the others sat outside it.

"Come," Fudenojo said. "Come outside, my brother."

After more coaxing, Juusuke came out of the cave. He looked around and smiled blissfully. "The cherry trees are in bloom," he said. "Are they not beautiful?" After a few minutes, he crawled back into the cave.

The others went separate ways, each to dwell with his sorrow about Juusuke in his own way. Manjiro sat down on a rock and wept. When the crying was done, his thoughts turned to home, to the fireflies and cherry blossoms Juusuke saw in his delirium, and to his family. He pictured his mother arranging flowers to place on the *tokonoma*, the home's "place of beauty," then moving to the family altar, the *butsudan*, to pray.

Manjiro whispered, "I am not dead, Okaasan. *Anshin shite kudasai*." (Don't worry.)

In his mind's eye, his little sister was also very sad. It must have hurt his older brother that from the time she had been able to walk, it had been Manjiro she followed around. Manjiro she looked to when her kite would not fly.

By tradition the oldest son in a family should have been registered as the head of household. But even before Manjiro was born, their mother said, she had known her first son would always need someone to take care of him. By now his mother had probably adopted a boy to take his place as head of household.

He suddenly sat bolt upright. The rock he was sitting on had trembled! Perhaps he had only imagined it. Seconds later it was as if something hit the island, jolted it. His insides slid in a sickening lurch. He had experienced this before. An earthquake!

The sea churned; rocks rolled and crashed against each other. Would the island sink?

The earthquake stopped. Fudenojo was calling.

"The cave is sealed!" Fudenojo shouted. "Juusuke

is trapped!" Frantically they wrestled loose rocks away from the entrance. Goemon sobbed aloud.

When they had removed enough of the stones to make a partial opening, Juusuke said, "This is a very sturdy cave."

Gritty dust and pebbles had fallen on him, but he had not even suffered a bruise.

4

A Desperate Situation

Juusuke's sudden clearness of mind did not last, and he often did not know where he was. Sometimes he crawled out of the cave, looked around, and asked, "Where is everybody? Have all abandoned us?"

As they began the fifth month on the island, Fudenojo climbed the rocks on the high end of the island. Since it was now summer, he hoped to find plants growing from windblown seed. Standing with Goemon, Manjiro watched Fudenojo move higher and higher.

Fudenojo had slipped! He was falling! Well above

where Manjiro and Goemon stood, Fudenojo hit a ledge with a thud.

For a stunned second, Manjiro couldn't move. Then he began to climb, scrambling toward the ledge. Goemon was right behind him, sobbing as he climbed.

When they reached the ledge, Fudenojo lay still and silent, his eyes closed.

"He's dead," Goemon wailed. "My brother is dead."

"Be quiet, Goemon!" Manjiro said, more sharply than he had meant to. Fudenojo was breathing, his chest rising and falling. If he was hurt badly enough that he could make the choice between life and death, Goemon's wailing of the word "dead" might lead him through that door.

"Fudenojo," Manjiro said in a calm voice, "you fell. Goemon and Manjiro are here. Open your eyes, please."

Fudenojo groaned, his eyes fluttered open, then closed again. "Loose rock," he mumbled.

Manjiro checked Fudenojo's arms and legs. Gashes were bleeding, and bruise welts were rising and turning purple. "Can you move your limbs?"

Tears still ran down Goemon's face, but he made no sound.

"No bones are broken," Fudenojo said. "I am just tired. So tired."

After the fall, Fudenojo spent more and more time in the cave with Juusuke. When he came outside, he gazed into space. His beard was so long now, and his eyes so sunken, that he made Manjiro think of the wise old man in Nakanohama.

With both his older brothers sick, Goemon sank into despair and wandered listlessly.

Manjiro found food for all of them and told them the things he had discovered. "Placing the seaweed on a rock and scraping it with your hand removes more of the salt than shaking does," he said.

He tried and tried but could not catch fish with his bare hands. Turtle! Turtles didn't react as quickly as fish did. He squatted and waited without moving until a turtle waded up from the water's edge to sun itself. Then he pounced quickly before it could return to the water, and safety.

With sharp stones, he and Toraemon removed the shell and gutted the turtle, then cut it up and gave each of the others a piece. After they managed to tear off and chew and swallow a bite, Manjiro said, "Raw turtle is as tough as raw albatross, but I think it is tastier."

No one responded.

"Do you not agree, Fudenojo, that turtle is tastier?"

Fudenojo looked at him as if he did not comprehend the question and said nothing.

When the meal, which they ate at midafternoon, was finished, Manjiro walked away from the others and stood alone. The sea stroked the rocks gently today; the murmur was like music. Or a poem. A poem

Manjiro had heard recited when he went to school at the Buddhist temple—before his father's death—came up from his mind's depths:

> The windblown
> Smoke of Mount Fuji
> Disappearing far beyond!
> Who knows the destiny
> Of my thought wandering away with it.

Here one's thought wandered away on ocean waves. The thought was strong and clear: I am the leader now. It did not please him, but neither did it frighten him.

5
A Ship

According to Fudenojo's marks on the drift-wood, they were into the sixth month on the island. Toraemon continued to help look for food, but he seemed to have given up hope that they would be rescued. Only Manjiro went each day to watch for a ship.

He went to his post with morning's first light because it was cooler then. The climbing walk did not make him as thirsty or tax his strength as much as it would if he waited until the sun beat down on the rocks.

This day, he watched the sun rise and trim white cloud streaks with gold, then dissolve the clouds as it inched up in the sky. The sea was serene; it reflected the sky's deepening blue. Manjiro squinted and shook his head. Was he imagining things, or did he see fountains of water spurting up? Yes! *Kujira!* Whales! He started to rise and go tell the others, then stopped. Why? Why waste his energy? What did *kujira* mean here? At home, a fisherman who spotted *kujira* would have rowed swiftly back toward shore and shouted the news. Then, amidst cries of *"Sore ike! Yare ike!"* a fleet of twenty or more boats filled with men and harpoons, ropes and floats, would set forth.

He had heard many stories about bringing in *kujira*, but in his part of Shikoku it had happened only twice in his memory. How wonderful it had been. Everyone in his village, and nearby villages—perhaps in the whole province of Tosa—had been excited and happy. The tantalizing smell of the steaks cooking over a charcoal fire . . .

Manjiro gritted his teeth and wiped his hand across his mouth. He must stop thinking of food.

The *kujira* were leaving. Good. He would not tell the others about the sighting. It would only make them sad. It would only make their stomachs rumble and spasm as his did now.

Ten days later, when Manjiro forced himself to walk what now seemed like a long way between the cave and the lookout point, he saw a speck far out on the water. A ship! But perhaps he only wished it to be a ship. Perhaps his imagination was trying to keep him from falling into the despair that had claimed his friends.

Using his hand as a shade over his eyes, he gazed at the speck. It was moving! It *was* a ship!

He walked as fast as he could back toward the cave and saw Goemon and Toraemon coming out of it. "A ship," he called. "Come quickly."

Goemon and Toraemon were so weak that they walked with effort, but they came. When they were there, looking out to sea, Goemon shook his head. "I don't see anything."

"Look," Manjiro said. "Do you see it now? It is coming this way."

"It is a ship!" Goemon said. "You can see its sails."

The ship turned in another direction and began to move away from them. *"Shikata ga nai,"* Toraemon said dully. (It can't be helped.)

Manjiro sat with his back straight, the sole of his left foot against his inner right thigh, his hands resting on his knees. Waiting, he thought only of not thinking; all was in Buddha's hands. Toraemon and Goemon stayed with him. Near noon the ship turned and came toward them again.

"Arigataya, arigataya," Manjiro whispered in thanksgiving. He stood, took their signal flag from its rock-wedged anchor, and began waving it.

6
Rescue

The ship stopped and lowered two boats. "Barbarians," Toraemon said in a low voice when the boats were close enough that they could see its occupants. "Three are light-skinned, and one is dark."

Manjiro recalled the wise man's reference to the barbarians as "blue-eyed sons of pigs," and his saying that they had hairy faces. He could not tell the color of their eyes from here, but one of them had a great deal of hair on his face.

A shiver ran down Manjiro's spine. These men might

kill them. But without further hesitation, he left the high point, with its steep drop to the sea, and started walking toward a gentler slope. Surely no death could be worse than the one they faced on this island.

When he reached the water's edge, he jumped in, swam to the nearest boat, and climbed in, bowing and thanking the men. Vaguely he realized that they were staring at him in open-mouthed astonishment.

When he looked fully at them, he saw that two did indeed have blue eyes, albeit different shades of blue. But one of the light-skinned men had brown eyes, and the dark-skinned man's eyes were also brown.

Toraemon and Goemon clambered into the boat, thanking the rescuers and telling about being caught in a storm.

The sailors, Manjiro realized, understood nothing they said. What if they rowed away without also rescuing Fudenojo and Juusuke? He gestured toward the island, pointed at his foot, and mimicked a limp, then started climbing out of the boat.

With his own gestures, the bearded man indicated that he understood and asked where they could get the boats into shore near the others.

Toraemon directed them to a point not far from the cave. But since Manjiro was the ablest of the three, he got out of the boat to lead the way to the cave.

Two sailors stayed, one in each boat. The other two—one of the light-skinned men, and the dark-skinned man, both of whom looked like giants when they stood up—followed Manjiro.   In response to his call, Fudenojo came out of the cave.   Then Juusuke came out and began crawling toward the boats.   The dark-skinned man picked Juusuke up in his arms and carried him.

Manjiro gasped when the boats drew close to the ship.   It was enormous, a three-masted ship with many sails.   Its flag had red and white stripes, and stars in one corner.

When they were on deck, Manjiro, shivering convulsively from fear and overexertion, immediately decided which of the men was master of this ship.   Not only his clothing but his demeanor marked the fair-skinned man with the strong jaw as the captain.   But the master of the ship was not looking at him—he was looking at Fudenojo, the only other member of their group still standing.   Toraemon, Juusuke, and Goemon had dropped to the deck and prostrated themselves before the ship's captain.

Fudenojo bowed and thanked the ship's captain and said in a clear voice that they were from the province of Tosa, and their boat had been wrecked in a storm.

For a fleeting moment, Manjiro resented Fudenojo's action.   He, Manjiro, had taken care of all of them these past few weeks!   He had been the leader!   In the next instant he sank to the deck, just before Fudenojo swayed and two sailors reached out to support him.   Manjiro trembled.   In his pride and conceit, he had wanted recognition, and he would have done a terrible thing. Even from the time he was a child, he had known the rule of the sea that captains addressed each other. He would have shamed Fudenojo—and himself.

The ship's master spoke with a firm, commanding voice, and when Manjiro glanced up, he understood that he and his friends were being told to rise.

They were each given a half cup of water. With his eyes, Manjiro asked the captain for more, but he shook his head and spoke to some of the sailors, who picked up the castaways, put them across their shoulders, carried them down to a room, and placed them on a bench beside a table. Manjiro's feet did not reach the floor. It was a torturous position.

His heart thumping wildly, he lowered his head and sat wondering what the barbarians intended to do with them. Barbarians were supposedly simpleminded, but perhaps they were not as simpleminded as his countrymen thought they were. Perhaps they had devised a clever, and cruel, method of torture. He could smell food, but they had not been given any. He could not stop a humiliating drooling.

The aroma became stronger. Manjiro looked up. They were not being tortured. A man was bringing food to them! But surely they were not to eat here, with their feet dangling above the floor. Yes, that was the intent. Evidently these people ate in this miserable position. Manjiro's pounding heart quieted.

The sailor brought dishes of steaming sweet potatoes. The barbarians must eat with the strange-looking tools that another man had placed beside their bowls. Manjiro picked them up in one hand and tried to make them work together to lift a bite of sweet potatoes.

The sailor who had brought the utensils took them from his hand and laid one of them aside, then demonstrated how to eat the potatoes with the other one, the one with prongs.

Ah, like a shovel, Manjiro thought. It worked! It worked well! And he had never tasted anything more delicious than these sweet potatoes.

The bowls were taken away. But he was still hungry. He knew the others were, too. So this was it. These men knew they were suffering terribly for want of water and food. First the barbarians gave their wretched victims only a half cup of water. Then they teased with only a portion of the food a starving man craves.

Again Manjiro and his friends sat with their heads bowed. No one had given a sign that they could rise.

After a time, the man who had brought the sweet potatoes came again, this time with bowls of soup. The soup reassured Manjiro. But what strange eating customs these people had—first sweet potatoes, then soup, with a long interval between.

The soup, which had chunks of meat in it, was satisfying and delicious. But Manjiro was still hungry when they were told to get up.

Later they were bidden back to the table, and this time the servers brought bowls of rice. Manjiro's eyes filled with tears. The wise man had been wrong. These people were not barbarians; they were kind—and they ate rice.

7
Difficult Adjustments

"Hammock," a sailor said to Manjiro. The sailor closed his eyes and laid the side of his face against his folded hands.

The men had strung other hammocks for Toraemon and Goemon. Juusuke, because of his injured foot, was assigned a bottom bunk. Fudenojo would sleep in a spare top bunk.

Manjiro was looking around the area that was evidently the sailors' home on the ship—the place where they ate and slept and did their mending—when powerful arms picked him up and put him on the hammock.

In the glow of lamplight, some of the sailors smoked pipes with long, slender handles while they talked. One of the dark men had a round box that made music when he squeezed its ends together. At first the music was merry, then it became filled with longing. Like him, Manjiro thought, these men were homesick.

Beneath his closed lids, his eyes stung, and his throat ached from locked-in weeping. From the day of the storm, survival had taken precedence over all else. Now that they were safe, the longing for home, for his family and his village, for flowers, for Nakanohama's gnarled old pine trees, and the comforting spirits of his ancestors, was almost too much to bear.

But he had to bear it. He didn't want their rescuers to think he was ungrateful. Besides, if he began to cry, Goemon would cry too. Manjiro took deep, even breaths. They were sailing in a light breeze; the hammock rocked gently. The pain in his chest slowly dissolved, and he felt himself sinking into sleep.

He awakened more than once before morning. The lamps that hung here and there, he realized, were always lit during dark hours. Some men would leave, yawning and stretching and mumbling; another group would come in. Manjiro thought almost longingly about the silent darkness of the cave.

The next day, when he and his Tosa friends were alone, Fudenojo said, "I had a reason for telling the

captain only that we are from the province of Tosa. I
suspect that means nothing to him. We must not speak
the name of our country."

Manjiro understood the wisdom of Fudenojo's
instructions. Even if the men on the ship were not barbarians, they were not Chinese, and they surely were
not Dutch. The wise old man had said all Dutchmen
were fat. Therefore, the men of this ship must be from
a country that was an enemy to Dai Nippon.

A week had passed since their rescue, and they
had been well treated, but Manjiro didn't think he had
ever been more miserable. Standing on the forecastle
deck with Goemon and Toraemon and Fudenojo, he
squirmed and grimaced.

"The captain is generous," Fudenojo said.

They had been given sea chests for their ragged
clothing, and provided with clothes like the sailors wore.

Manjiro knew Fudenojo did right to mention the
generosity, but the clothing was so uncomfortable that
his mood had turned sour. The checked shirt was not
bad, but nothing good could be said of the pants and
footwear. The pants flared out below the knees, but
were so tight across the buttocks and thighs that one
could not squat, or sit in the comfortable half-lotus
position. The shoes were worse. They were devices

of torture. Manjiro shifted from one foot to the other. "These people," he said, "must be strong to bear such pain without complaint."

"Yes," Goemon said. "I almost envy Juusuke. He only has to wear one of the miserable things. Never before did I so appreciate the joy of bare feet or straw sandals."

Toraemon gave one of his slightly mocking grins. "Are these the same two who a few days ago constantly spoke of their gratitude to their rescuers?"

Manjiro looked down at the deck. Toraemon was right; he and Goemon should be ashamed. "We are forever in the Mr. Aiken's debt for what he has done for Juusuke," he said. Mr. Aiken, the chief mate, had applied medicine, then plaster and bandages to Juusuke's injured foot.

When Goemon did not take the opportunity to unburden his spirit of the critical words he had spoken about their benefactors, Manjiro added, "And I'm sure Goemon agrees that the Mr. Rosten was very kind to cut our hair and loan us scissors to cut our toenails and fingernails." Mr. Rosten, who made barrels for some purpose, had also shaved off Fudenojo's long, ragged goatee.

"Yes, that was most kind," Goemon said a bit sullenly.

Like Mr. Rosten, Manjiro thought, all the sailors seemed to have more than one skill. For instance, every man of the crew took a turn at the wheel, which meant that all knew how to steer the big ship.

When they were working, they did not talk much. But when they were not on duty, they used many more words than Nihonjin did. Even when one's feelings about something could be conveyed with a look or a grunt, the sailors chose to speak. Sometimes two men would speak to each other with angry voices. And once two sailors not much older than Goemon had bloodied each other with their fists.

Manjiro had been watching them and had been greatly startled when Captain Whitfield himself shouted from the elevated deck where he walked, "Avast, Jerry McKay! Avast, Cliff Wixson!"

The fighting had immediately stopped; fighters and onlookers had silently gone their separate ways. Surely the captain of a great ship was like a lord, Manjiro thought. Why then had he stopped the fight himself instead of telling one of those who served him to do so? Why had the men not been punished?

And, strangest of all, how was it that the next day the two who had been fighting were talking together?

Manjiro moved his eyes from the bottom to the top of the rigging. Always men were up there with buckets and brushes. Others were replacing or repairing something that had to do with the sails and sheets. When they lifted their eyes from their work, they looked for something out there in the water.

On each of the three masts, a man stood high above

the deck not working at all. Those men did nothing but search the waves with a long instrument held up to one eye.

Manjiro surmised that what the sailors searched for had something to do with the enormous brick structure between the fore and the mainmast. Each of the two iron pots in the brick housing was big enough to cook a grandfather sea turtle. Often men were down inside them scouring them until they shone like silver.

By the end of the second week, he understood that the men were searching for something called "whales."

"The purpose of the brick structure with its pots is to cook whales," he told his friends. "That is what the sailors with sharp eyes are looking for."

"How do you know this?" Fudenojo asked. "You cannot understand their language."

"They speak with their hands and faces just as we do," Manjiro said. "They often say 'whales.' And when they are on deck and say 'whales,' they are apt to glance at the pots."

"And what is 'whales'?"

"I think it is their word for *kujira*," Manjiro said.

Fudenojo scowled. "All on board ship could not eat even one before it spoiled."

Manjiro sighed. What Fudenojo said was true, which meant that his careful observations had evidently led him to a wrong conclusion. Not being able to understand their rescuers' language was very trying.

With the passing days, Manjiro's admiration for the sailors increased. The drinking water supply was short, and water was strictly rationed. That was why he and his friends had been given only half a cup of water the day they were rescued. "These men perspire a great deal," he said to Goemon. "But they do not complain that they do not have enough water."

While he considered chopsticks preferable and superior to knives and forks, he soon learned to use the sailors' eating utensils. He and his friends were now served portions of different foods on one plate instead of small portions with long intervals between servings. They still didn't know why they had been served that way when they were first rescued. Manjiro could understand some of what the sailors said, but he couldn't speak enough words in their language to ask such questions.

A boy named Billy was helping him to learn new words. Billy was taller and huskier than Goemon, but he had told Manjiro he was fifteen, Manjiro's age. Billy's eyes were blue, but he in no way resembled the image of a barbarian Manjiro had held from the old wise man's stories about them. Billy's hair was the color of new straw sandals, and his ears were like small wings. Brown spots of different shapes and sizes dotted his face.

Manjiro had observed all that when Billy first came up to him, tapped his own chest, and said, "Billy."

Manjiro tapped his chest. "Manjiro."

Billy indicated the flag with red and white stripes and stars in the corner, brought his hand back to his chest. "American."

Remembering Fudenojo's instructions, Manjiro said, "Tosa."

Billy had shaken his head and said words Manjiro knew meant that Billy had never heard of his country. He didn't tell Billy that he had never heard of his homeland either. That would not be polite.

The name of the ship was the *John Howland*. Manjiro had no trouble with "John," but "Howland" came out "Howrand." Nor could he say "Honolulu," Billy's favorite place away from home, the way Billy said it. It came out "Honoruru" no matter how hard he tried; there simply was no "l" sound in his language.

With words, signs, and drawings, Billy explained that the huge brick structure with its iron pots was used to cook the oil out of whales.

Manjiro smiled to himself when Billy drew a picture of a whale. He had been right when he told Fudenojo and the others that he thought "whales" was their rescuers' word for *kujira*.

Whaling was a big business for America and other countries, Billy told Manjiro. The oil was used for lamps and candles, and to make machines operate efficiently. There were already many barrels of oil in the hold, Billy said. Jesse Rosten, who made the barrels

on board the ship, was called a cooper.

With signs and facial expressions to go with the words, Billy told Manjiro that one kind of whale—the sperm whale—had something in its intestines called ambergris. "It's used to make real expensive perfume. We sight a sperm whale, you'll know by the cheering. And how scared we are. They can be mean."

When they returned to America and sold the oil and ambergris, Billy explained, all on board would share in the profits.

Some of the men were teaching Manjiro how to climb the rigging. It was not as easy as it looked. The higher one went, the more pronounced the ship's roll became. It was exciting, though, and he didn't understand why his friends preferred to stand around on the forecastle deck in each other's company.

Perhaps, he thought as he stood on a swaying yard, he would see a big school of whales, as he had that day when he and his Tosa friends were on the rock island. Captain Whitfield would be pleased with him if he did.

8
John Mung

Manjiro gave up on going back to sleep. It was as if the August sun that had beat down through the day had been trapped in their quarters, which were stifling even at best.

A bell had struck not long ago. Soon after he and his friends had come aboard, Manjiro had come to understand that the bells marked the time. He now knew that the men were divided into two watches, the starboard watch and the larboard watch. The watches were on duty for four-hour stretches, except for the early morning two-hour "dog watch." But since he did not know the hour the bells indicated, he did not know whether the night had much or little time left.

He swung down from his hammock, stood with his feet planted apart until he adjusted to the ship's roll, went past the restless men and up the forecastle companionway, slid open the scuttle slide, and stepped onto the deck. There was no moon, but the stars were so brilliant the lanterns looked wan by comparison. Scanning the heavens to check the positions of the constellations, he decided it was not long, perhaps an hour, before daybreak.

This was much better, he thought as he went across the deck to the bulwark. The sound of water rushing against the hull and the hum of the breeze in the rigging were restful. One of the men on duty cleared his throat, another sang quietly.

Manjiro waited. His eyelids were heavy now, but it would only be a little longer; the stars were fading.

It became very dark. There, day was breaking to the fore of the ship, the first gray streaks spreading across the horizon. Then came that strange light on the sea that filled him with longing and loneliness.

Someone was walking in the light. Shadowy as the image was, Manjiro recognized the male figure. It was himself. But an older self, a man grown. His mother was walking toward him. She was older too; gray streaked her hair. Manjiro felt himself slipping down onto the deck, felt the sleep-breathing that kept time with the ship's rocking.

A shout awakened him. The two words "There blows!" echoed in his ears as he got to his feet.

The sun was up, and a man high in the rigging again called, "There blows," his voice ringing with excitement.

Billy, a big smile spread across his face, ran past Manjiro. "Whales," Billy said.

Manjiro ran to catch up with Billy. Others were running about. Captain Whitfield called to the man who had spotted the whales, "Where away?"

There were more questions and answers between the captain and the sailor who saw the whales. Then Manjiro heard the call, "Lower away!"

Jake, one of the men who had come in a whaling boat to rescue them from the rock island, was going after a whale. So was Benjamin, the dark-skinned man who had carried Juusuke to the boat, and Ira Davis, an intense, somewhat nervous man.

"Harpooneers," Billy said.

The harpooneers chanted as they left. Manjiro caught none of the words, but he sensed that those on board worried for the men going out to kill a whale.

While he and Billy stood facing the bow, Captain Whitfield called orders and the yards swung to the left. "Larboard," Billy said. The yards swung to the right. "Starboard," Billy said. The men sang out to the sheets as they took in sail.

The *John Howland*, Manjiro realized, had to stay reasonably close to the whaling boats, but not so close that it interfered with the chase.

Now and then, Captain Whitfield, with the long glass to his eye, gave a report. When a cheer went up, Manjiro knew that a whale had been killed, and that the men in the boats were safe.

A hush fell among the crew, and Toraemon, at Manjiro's side, said, "After the victory comes the remorse."

Manjiro knew what Toraemon meant. He had experienced the exhilaration of bringing in a big fish. And had known that moment of pain for taking its life. He had always thought it was because of the teaching that all beings were Buddha beings. But now, just as Toraemon said, he saw the fleeting identity with the whale in the faces of these men who knew nothing of Buddha.

The boats were coming now with the dead whale in tow. In its wake, a red stain colored the water. The ship lay at a standstill, lowering and raising its bow as if it were impatient to be on its way again.

With his Tosa friends, Manjiro watched men lash the enormous, open-eyed corpse to the side of the ship.

"Do you remember the saying that one whale means a time of riches for all of Tosa?" Fudenojo asked. "But we on Tosa do not have the boats nor the tools these men have for whaling."

The thought came swiftly into Manjiro's mind: I will

learn about the boats and harpoons and how to get oil from the whale. And what I will learn will help our people. He pictured their faces as he told them about whaling. The farmer whose rice he had polished would be there, and the old wise man, and the fishermen. They would all be listening attentively, nodding now and then. At the fringe of the group would stand his mother, smiling proudly.

Manjiro drew in his breath. In the time before sunrise, he had a vision—or a dream—of meeting his mother. And just now he had pictured himself telling the people of his village about whaling. Surely this meant that he would return to his homeland.

He closed his eyes and tried to recapture the details of the vision. Perhaps it had not been a vision at all. The sea at first break of day had cast a spell over him, and his hope of returning home had made itself into a dream.

He opened his eyes and straightened his shoulders. But the thought that he would learn about whaling so he could help his people was not a dream. That was purpose.

Mentally recording each step, he watched men lower two narrow platforms partway down the side of the hull to a point above the whale. Men—secured by ropes to keep them from falling amidst the sharks the dead whale had attracted—went down to the platforms. The men had sharp-pointed knives on long handles.

Beginning behind the whale's nose, they cut a spiral from its flesh in a continuous strip.

Men raised the great strips of whale flesh onto the deck; others cut the flesh into blocks for boiling the fat out in the huge pots. The fire had been started with wood, but now the crisp, cooked-out pieces of flesh and fat were the fuel. With slings and tackles, other men took barrels of oil to the hold.

All through that day and the next day, and into the third day, Manjiro would sleep a while, then go to watch again. Between the stench of the whale's rotting flesh and the stench of the smoke, he became so sick to his stomach he couldn't eat.

"Why do you punish yourself like this?" Fudenojo asked. "It is foolish."

"I want to learn."

Fudenojo shook his head. "What is there to learn the third day that you did not learn the first day?"

There was always something new to learn, Manjiro thought. But if he said that, it would sound as if he were being critical of his Tosa friends. "Sometimes my attention has wandered," he said instead.

When all was done, very little of the whale went to the sharks. Even the whale's ashes would be used to make soap to scrub down the oily decks, Billy told Manjiro.

Although he still could not converse much with the sailors, Manjiro now understood most of what was said. One day, he heard the sailors talking about a country called Japan. "They call us barbarians," one of the men said.

Manjiro sat very still. The country they called Japan must be Dai Nippon. And these men *were* among those his countrymen called barbarians.

Another man told how one of America's crippled ships had put into port on a small Japanese island. "They put our men in jail," he said. "And when they escaped, the black-hearted knaves put them in cages!"

Chill bumps broke out on Manjiro's arms. Fudenojo had been wise to choose not to tell the name of their country. And he, Manjiro, had been wise to listen and learn without talking about his own life.

As time passed, he became increasingly restless. He wanted to work, but he knew he must wait for Fudenojo to approach the captain.

Manjiro paced. He sighed. He said, "I am getting fat."

"We need to work," Fudenojo finally said. "I will speak to Captain Whitfield." He started toward the captain.

Manjiro cleared his throat. "When the captain is on the quarterdeck, we must ask the officer of the deck's permission to speak with him," he said.

Fudenojo stopped walking and looked at him in surprise. Fudenojo, Manjiro realized, had not observed the procedure. He was glad he had spoken up.

Fudenojo would have been embarrassed when he later realized that he had not acted according to the Americans' protocol.

Fudenojo spoke to Mr. Burke. When Fudenojo had gained permission, he approached Captain Whitfield.

Manjiro could not put all Fudenojo had said about feeling unworthy and desiring to help into the captain's language. He only said, "Wish work, please."

Captain Whitfield did not look at Manjiro. He looked directly at Fudenojo. Then he shook Fudenojo's hand.

How wise this Captain Whitfield is, Manjiro thought.

Early the next morning, he and his friends began to work with other men at the daily chore of cleaning and swabbing the decks. They knotted yarns and scraped rust from the chain cables. Manjiro was now comfortable enough in the sail rigging that he was allowed to help with the endless upkeep and repair.

But since they were not assigned to a watch, they still had free time. Captain Whitfield gave them permission to wander anywhere they liked.

One afternoon they went down in the hold and saw cows and pigs there. Manjiro held his face expressionless when he realized that the two men who tended the animals—and no doubt slaughtered those that became the meat the cook prepared—ate and slept in the same quarters with the rest of the crew. In his country, men who slaughtered animals were *etta* (filled with filth). Because they did un-Buddhist work, no one associated with them. It was as if they were invisible.

Manjiro knew the others were as horrified as he. He also knew they would never discuss the matter with each other nor give any indication of their feelings about eating with *etta*.

America, he thought, evidently had no caste system. *Etta* were not shunned. Officers talked and laughed with sailors in lowly positions. When he and Billy had a learning session, Manjiro sketched a ship with an American flag, except he only put one big star on the flag. On the ship's deck, he drew figures of officers and cook and greenhands standing side by side, all smiling.

Billy snorted. Then, with pictures and words, he told Manjiro that he and his friends were lucky to get picked up by Captain Whitfield. On most ships, Billy told him, the after gang, which included all officers, didn't mix with forecastle men. "But on the *John Howland*, everybody mixes free and easy."

Manjiro nodded. On board ship, the association between officers and crew depended on the captain. But that did not explain the system in America, and he didn't know how to make his question clear.

"On the *John Howland*, even the captain's door is open to everybody," Billy said. He put his fingers on Manjiro's chest. "Including you."

At first Manjiro went timidly to Captain Whitfield's cabin. Captain Whitfield seemed to welcome his visit.

He began to go more and more often to see the captain. He liked the smell of ink and paper and varnished wood. He liked the quiet. He did not always mind the men's talk and laughter and swearing, but sometimes his ears pleaded for rest.

The captain's charts intrigued him, as did a colorful round globe on a pedestal. The captain said the instruments in a rack were guns—rifles and pistols—but the ammunition was under lock and key. "We have never had occasion to use them," Captain Whitfield said. "And I pray we never do."

Once Manjiro went to the captain's open door and saw him looking at a photograph of a lady. The captain was crying. "Mrs. Whitfield," he said. "My wife."

"She is . . . ?"

"Yes," Captain Whitfield said. "She is dead."

"My father, too," Manjiro told him. He regretted again, as he had many times, that he had not gone to the cemetery and told his father that he was going fishing. He felt sad, and homesick, and very close to Captain Whitfield.

Not long after that visit, on a day when the sails drooped and small white clouds lazed across the sky, Mr. O'Brien, the second mate, told Manjiro he could go up and look for whales.

Standing on a crosstree, two narrow parallel sticks attached far above the deck to a mast, he searched the water for a spout, sometimes with his naked eyes, sometimes with the spyglass. For an hour he saw nothing. Then, through the glass, he saw a movement of water that didn't fit the wave pattern. Yes, a funnel-shaped spume! Pointing, he called, "There blows."

A minute later, someone in the rigging shouted, "Sperm whale!"

Manjiro looked down at the deck, saw men dancing with excitement, and remembered what Billy had told him about sperm whales. He had spotted the whale with expensive perfume in its intestines!

When at last the boats returned with an enormous whale in tow, there was much rejoicing. Captain Whitfield put a sailor's cap on Manjiro's head.

"A sailor on the *John Howland* should have a name we can pronounce," one of the men said.

"I have it!" another said. "John Mung."

"John Mung," the others agreed.

Manjiro smiled proudly. Not only had the crew given him the name of the ship, they had given him two names. He bowed and said, "John Mung thanks you."

Billy smiled wide. "See how good I've taught him to talk American," he said.

9
Typhoon!

After four months on the *John Howland*, Manjiro could get the gist of almost anything the men said, although he still found the various forms of speech mystifying. Some used *thee* and *thou* while others did not. And some, Billy told him, were immigrants who had not yet learned to "talk American good."

Other than his difficulties with the language, Manjiro felt as if he were now a part of the crew. On this morning, he and his Tosa friends had just finished helping to clean the decks when the seven bells for breakfast sounded. He didn't say anything to the others, but an uneasiness prickled his scalp. The breeze and the sea seemed restless. He scanned the sky. The sun looked brassy, but there were no threatening clouds.

Since he was not part of a regular watch, he went down to breakfast, then came back up on deck. Clouds were now swelling on the horizon; the air and sea had an ominous feel about them. Captain Whitfield was on deck, his calm voice calling orders to the men aloft. Other men were raising the whaling boats higher up the hull and lashing them.

Klaus Eich, the carpenter, stood on the forecastle deck gazing at the building clouds and said, "Ve vill get blow."

"Pacific means peaceful," Jake said from behind Manjiro. "But it don't always live up to its name." He sounded excited.

Why was Jake up here? Manjiro wondered. Jake was not on this watch. He was supposed to be resting.

Jake stepped up beside Manjiro, grinned and rubbed his hands together. "Here it comes."

The clouds came suddenly, racing, billowing, blacking out sun and sky.

Mr. Aiken ran to the forecastle hatchway and shouted, "All hands! Tumble up here!"

"And take in sail, me hearties," Jake said to no one in particular. "You can go below if you want to, John."

Frightened as he was just standing on the pitching

deck, Manjiro shook his head and ran with Jake. He was part of the crew; he knew how to take in sail.

"Lower top mizzen sail," Jake said. "I'm right behind you."

An eerie twilight closed around Manjiro as he crawled out on a yard. It was all right; he had been a lot higher than this. Thunder crashed, and lightning bolts linked monstrous black waves to the blackness from whence they came. The wind howled; rain came down like a slanting, blinding waterfall. Then the bucking ship tilted almost on its side.

Manjiro gasped, lay out across the yard, and held on.

The ship came upright again. He had to get up from here. He had to help Jake. But his body would not obey. He couldn't turn loose. He was shaking violently, and he was sick. He was going to vomit; he couldn't hold it back. There it went with the wind.

The ship rolled again. Manjiro clenched his jaws to keep from screaming. His hands were moving now, they were working with the sail. They seemed to be detached from the rest of his body. No, please, no. He was going to be sick again.

Something was poking him. Jake. Jake was poking him hard, motioning for him to come down. From somewhere he heard the wind-borne call, "All snug aloft!"

When he was back on the deck, Manjiro kept his eyes lowered. Even now his body could not forget its terror. A rigor would go through him and he would think that was it, that the shaking was over, then it would hit again.

"Go 'tween decks," Jake said through cupped hands into his ear, so his words would not be lost in the wind and rain, the pounding against the hull, the screeching of the swaying masts.

Manjiro soon realized why Jake had said to go between decks, where provisions were kept. It was more stable there than in the forecastle. The storm, a sailor told Manjiro, was a typhoon. "It's an old grandpa typhoon, though," he said. "Weak and tired out."

Manjiro thought that if this was a grandpa typhoon, he was glad it had not visited them when it was young and strong. The *John Howland* bucked and rolled. Stirred-up bilge water, the water that collected in the ship's bottom and became foul, filled the ship with a stink.

Being between decks helped; Fudenojo's advice to drink nothing but tea, and to eat nothing but hardtack, helped. Still, Manjiro was sick to his stomach. He was even sicker at heart. Jake obviously had not told the others about his cowardice, how he had clung to the yard and been of little help. But he knew. He would have to live with his shame.

At last the sea became calm. Sails went up, filled, and gleamed white in sparkling sunshine.

In the forecastle, the men smoked the long-stemmed pipes called tomahawks and drank tea and talked. Manjiro listened with downcast eyes to stories about gales and typhoons, and ice storms around Cape Horn. Then the men told about how terrified they had been the first time they went aloft during a bad blow. "I laid myself out on a yard and stuck like glue," Jake said.

The men laughed, and one of them said, "How ye react the first time be not the test. The test be the willingness to go at all."

Manjiro lifted his head. And Jake lifted his cup of tea. "To John Mung—a true sailor," he said.

10
Honolulu

Manjiro and his friends had been aboard the *John Howland* for five and a half months when the ship approached Honolulu. Captain Whitfield had told Manjiro that Honolulu was a port city on the island of Oahu. "Oahu is the main island of the kingdom of Hawaii, a good friend to the United States," he had said.

When Manjiro went below, then came back topside, the *John Howland* wallowed at anchor, well out from the port. "So many ships," he said in a low, awed voice.

Hundreds of merchant ships and whaling ships from many countries lay at anchor side by side.

Billy came up to him. "Wind's out," he said. "We can't get in yet. While we're waiting, Cap'n Whitfield's gone ashore to make arrangements for you and the others to stay in Honolulu."

It saddened Manjiro that he would have to bid farewell to the men of the *John Howland*. Many of them had become his good friends. And he had great affection for Captain Whitfield.

For two days and nights, he did not see Captain Whitfield. But when they were able to get into port, the captain himself escorted Manjiro and his friends onto shore.

All the activity made Manjiro dizzy. Crates of fruits and vegetables and other food supplies were being loaded into boats to be taken out to ships. Seamen wearing caps, breeches, and coats of various styles haggled with browned people wearing bright clothing.

And there, while one group of sailors made music, others danced with women! Merchant and whaling men spoke in a variety of languages, and some argued loudly. In his country, Manjiro had never been anywhere but to neighboring villages, but he had heard stories about cities where scowling samurai flashed their long swords if a crowd grew noisy. Here, no one made an effort to control the crowd. No one even gave way, much less bowed to another.

Manjiro edged closer to Captain Whitfield.

A pretty, smiling woman, with black hair so long it hung down her back, was coming toward them with a garland of flowers. She was smiling at Captain Whitfield. The captain was bending down to let her put the flowers around his neck!

Manjiro knew that behind his Tosa friends' unruffled expressions, they too were amazed, even horrified. No, Toraemon was not horrified. A tiny smile twitched at the corners of Toraemon's mouth and he said, *"Ii na... Urayamashii na!"* (Oh, to be Captain Whitfield.)

And Fudenojo, serious-minded Fudenojo, laughed at his friend's remark.

When he had guided them through the port into the town, where people ambled rather than rushing about, Captain Whitfield said, "The real Honolulu."

From the way he said it, Manjiro knew the captain had great affection for this town.

As they walked, tears came to Manjiro's eyes. How glorious the sight, how precious the smell of plants, from trees to the smallest flower. And no man-made music could match that of a songbird. But he heard a sound even more wonderful than the birds' songs: the laughter of children playing. His little sister and her friends laughed like that.

The captain brought them to a house where they met a man named Dr. Judd.

"Captain Whitfield has told me about your rescue,"

Dr. Judd said in a clipped, formal voice. He picked up a small sack, opened it, and dumped coins out on a table.

Manjiro couldn't help it; he sucked in his breath. The coins were like those used in his country! Unprepared, Fudenojo and Juusuke were also unable to mask their excitement.

"Ah," Dr. Judd said. "Dai Nippon Teikoku?"

Manjiro felt sick. This Dr. Judd knew the name of their country, and he had some of its coins. He must also know that their country had imprisoned ship-wrecked American sailors. Had even put some of them in cages. And Dr. Judd knew from their reactions that Dai Nippon was their homeland. Captain Whitfield would despise them now. And maybe they would be put in prison.

Fudenojo began to talk rapidly, to explain that they were poor fishermen, that they had been caught in a storm and that Kuroshio had taken them to a rocky, barren island.

When he paused for breath, Dr. Judd shook his head and lifted his hand, palm outward.

"I know only a few words of your language." He turned to Captain Whitfield. "You were right in your guess. They are Japanese."

Captain Whitfield had known!

Captain Whitfield nodded, then said, "John Mung understands English quite well."

"Ah," Dr. Judd said again, and looked at Manjiro.

"Then you can translate for your friends when I have finished."

Manjiro quickly became confused. He was not accustomed to Dr. Judd's voice, and Dr. Judd made long sentences and used strange words. While Manjiro pondered the words *anti-trading stance* and *prohibitive laws*, he lost what Dr. Judd said next. He picked up a brief sentence, "None are still here." The last part had something to do with the man to whom the coins had belonged, but he didn't understand what.

When Dr. Judd fell silent, Manjiro looked at Captain Whitfield. The captain's eyes twinkled, but he offered no help. Manjiro explained the part he had caught, the part that was important, to his friends. None of their countrymen were here.

"We have heard that Dutch ships go to our homeland," Fudenojo said. "Is there perhaps one in the harbor on which we could work our passage?"

When Manjiro translated, Dr. Judd stared at Fudenojo. "A Dutch captain would have to be a madman to take you to Japan!" he said. "And you . . ." He shook his head several times, as if Fudenojo were also mad.

Manjiro started to translate, but Fudenojo stopped him. *"Wakatta,"* he said. (I understand.)

Since it had taken concentration to translate from Japanese to English and back again, Manjiro didn't think until then about what Dr. Judd had said. Why would a Dutch captain have to be a madman to take

them to Japan? And why did Dr. Judd apparently consider Fudenojo crazy for trying to find a way for them
to go home? Did not all people love their homeland?

"Dr. Judd has found a place for you to live," Captain
Whitfield said to Manjiro and his friends.

"You need not concern yourselves about
expenses," Dr. Judd added. "The Hawaiian government will take care of them."

"Thank you for all you've done, Dr. Judd," Captain
Whitfield said. He turned to Manjiro and his friends.
"I have work to attend to now. We need to make
repairs and purchase provisions. We'll probably be
here for four weeks. I'll see you again before we sail."

11
A Decision

Manjiro liked the grass-roofed house, which seemed right for the agreeable weather. The December nights were pleasantly cool, the days pleasantly warm. Rains, sometimes hard rains, came, but most of the time the sun shone.

He also liked the town with its great palace, the lovely gardens that reminded him of home, and the trees, which included a majestic branchless tree with a crown of leaves at the top.

At first he kept expecting checkpoints where they

would be asked to show registration papers. And they had been given none. But as the days turned into a week, then two weeks, he realized that this land was totally opposite from Dai Nippon when it came to freedom of movement. There were no restrictions at all.

Sometimes they wandered for many miles in the beautiful valley behind Honolulu. *"Koko wa gokuraku,"* Manjiro heard Toraemon say. (It is paradise.)

Manjiro wanted to go down to the harbor to see Billy and some of the others, but when he mentioned it, Fudenojo said, "The captain told us they would be busy—a polite way of telling us not to bother them."

"It is even more important here than on the ship that we do not remain idle," Juusuke said.

"Yes," Fudenojo said. "We will ask Dr. Judd how to go about finding work."

When they went to see Dr. Judd, and Manjiro asked where they might find work, he said, "I'll keep it in mind. But there's no hurry."

No hurry, Manjiro thought. That might be the slogan for Honolulu. Once away from the harbor, no one seemed to be in a hurry.

The four weeks passed, and Captain Whitfield did not come back. Surely, Manjiro thought, he would come to say good-bye to them.

Early in the next week, Captain Whitfield came. After greeting them, he said, "I'd like to talk to you on a special matter, Fudenojo."

Fudenojo motioned for Manjiro to translate.

The captain used simple words and made short sentences that Manjiro had no trouble understanding, but it was not easy to translate from one language to another. In his concentration, he scarcely understood until Captain Whitfield's address to Fudenojo stopped.

At that point, the impact of the captain's request hit Manjiro. His heart pumped faster; his mind whirled. Captain Whitfield had asked if Manjiro could sail on the *John Howland* for the rest of its whaling trip—then go on to America!

He sensed the struggle inside Fudenojo. Fudenojo was responsible for him.

Did he want to go if Fudenojo gave permission? He and his friends had endured much together. They were more like brothers than friends.

But what an adventure it would be to go to America! And since Captain Whitfield was a whaler, it would not be like saying good-bye to his friends forever. Captain Whitfield had obviously been to Honolulu many times. Manjiro would see his friends when he and the captain returned here.

At last Fudenojo turned to Manjiro. "It is you who will stay or go. You must decide."

"I want to go," Manjiro said.

12
Far From Home

Another ship came into view, then sailed directly toward them. That ship, and then the *John Howland*, began to take in sail, and soon they lay with their bows almost touching.

Standing aport with Manjiro, Billy said, "It's the *Madison* we're speaking. Cap'n Whitfield's going over to make the gam with its captain, and its chief mate's coming over to make the gam with Mr. Aiken."

"What is a gam?" Manjiro asked.

"It's not *a* gam. It's *the* gam. Talk. That's how we

keep up with what's going on at different ports—and even back home."

Mr. Burke, the second mate, who had walked up, said, "It is also how we receive and send mail."

Manjiro nodded. Some of the crew had read over and over letters that had been waiting for them when they reached Honolulu.

"My older brother is a schoolteacher," Mr. Burke said. "I shall be glad to teach thee to read and write English, John. And thee too, Billy."

"I can read fine," Billy said stiffly. "Excuse me. I've got work to do."

Manjiro wondered if Billy really could read or write. He had not seen him reading a letter, or writing one. Billy only drew pictures.

"I will be most grateful," Manjiro said.

The next day, he went to Mr. Burke's quarters for his first lesson. Mr. Burke, who Manjiro thought was only a few years older than he, said, "Thou should first learn how to write thy name, date, and place of birth. Every time thou turnest around, thou will need to put that information on one form or another." He wrote letters. "It is thy name—John Mung."

Painstakingly, Manjiro copied the letters.

"I will do the rest in order that we have time left for thy lesson," Mr. Burke said. "Later thou must copy this and practice writing it. Place of birth?"

"Nakanohama," Manjiro said. "Province of Tosa.

Island of Shikoku. Dai Nippon." As he said it, a wave of longing went through him, not only for his family, but for his country. The people called his land Shimaguni, the island country, and Shimaguni's soul was *yamato damashi*. An indescribable loss lay within anyone who was separated from *yamato damashi*.

Mr. Burke moved his fingertips over the scars on his face, which Billy said were caused by a disease called smallpox. "Let us just make it Japan," he said. "Year of birth?"

"Year of the Boar." He did not add that the Year of the Boar was a year of courage. That would be boastful.

Mr. Burke cleared his throat. "How many years ago was the Year of the Boar?"

"It is fifteen years."

Manjiro watched Mr. Burke write down numbers. "The year of birth is 1827, John. Birthday?"

Birth day? Day of birth? In summer, his mother had told him, but she hadn't said when in summer.

Speaking very slowly, Mr. Burke asked, "John, on what day dost thou celebrate becoming a year older?"

Manjiro considered that question. In his country, the new year, and therefore, turning of age celebrations, lasted for five days. But Mr. Burke had asked for only one day. In Honolulu, American sailors had made much noise to greet their new year of 1842. But they did not celebrate on the following days. He smiled at Mr. Burke. "First day, new year."

As Mr. Burke wrote, he said, "Age, fifteen."

Before he realized that he was correcting his teacher, Manjiro said, "Sixteen."

"If these are correct dates, thou art *fifteen!*"

Manjiro nodded, although he knew he was right. The time in the womb counted as the first year. All babies turned two with the coming of the new year after their birth. He was sixteen.

Mr. Burke rose from his chair. "That's enough for today, John. Practice writing these words and numbers. Thou will need them in America. We will have another lesson tomorrow."

"Mr. Burke is good teacher," Manjiro told Billy.

Billy snorted. "You're so smart you've learned despite his bumbling. What you've done is make him decide he sure enough is a teacher. And it's not just me he's pestering to take lessons from him. You don't stop bragging on him, he'll open a dang school on the *John Howland*." Billy turned on his heel and walked away.

Manjiro sighed. He didn't understand how anybody could turn down an opportunity to learn. He didn't know why Billy was angry. To dolphins cavorting on the port side, he said, "You smile and play because your lives are simple."

It was not Mr. Burke, but the captain who gave Manjiro his first geography lesson.

"The world," Captain Whitfield said when they were in the captain's quarters, and Manjiro stood gazing at the colorful ball on a pedestal. "All the blue areas are oceans."

Manjiro's eyes flicked upward to the captain's face, then back to the globe. He knew now that the sea "out there" beyond his country's fishing waters was vast, but he had not imagined that water covered so much of the earth.

Captain Whitfield picked up a pointer and touched the globe. "Your country," he said.

It was so small. All the islands together took up only a tiny space.

Captain Whitfield turned the globe. "And here are the Americas." He started near the top with the pointer. "North America. Central America. South America."

Manjiro gasped. "America is big."

Captain Whitfield smiled. "These are the States, our part of the Americas, and this is called Spanish California, but to be more accurate, it is Mexican California. Now, see this small state. It has a long name. Massachusetts. That's home, John."

Manjiro heard the note of longing in Captain Whitfield's voice when he said, "That's home," and realized that the captain considered it Manjiro's home, too.

But it was not his home. His home was one of those Japanese islands. A village where ancient pines weathered storms, and flower gardens were a part of even the poorest hut. A house where his family lived, and where his ancestors were listed and honored.

Although he was aware that Captain Whitfield was watching him, Manjiro did not look up at his face.

"John, some things were meant to be," Captain Whitfield said. He put the pointer down, went to his desk, and opened his log book. "I'd like to read an entry to you," he said. "I wrote it the day we brought you and your friends on board." He read:

Sunday, June 27, 1841

This day light winds from the S.E. The Isle in sight 26 1:00 p.m. Sent in two boats to see if there were any turtles. Found 5 poor distressed people on the Isle. Took them off. Could not understand anything from them more than they were hungry. Made the latitude of the Isle 30 deg. 31 min. N.

Manjiro sucked in his breath. "You did not see the piece of canvas I waved? You did not come to rescue us? You only found us because the men were looking for turtles?"

"That is what we thought," Captain Whitfield said. "We spotted the isle, then went on our way. But one of the men said some turtle soup would make a fine Sunday supper. Turtles are found near islands. We turned back, cast anchor—and sent in the boats." Captain Whitfield paused, then went on. "But why did we have a sudden craving for turtle soup? And why did it happen to be on a Sunday, the Lord's day? Had it not been Sunday, we would not have stopped. God moves in mysterious ways."

Manjiro's head whirled. The things Captain Whitfield had said stirred him. But he did not understand. Who was this God Captain Whitfield and the men often referred to and spoke with? This God who had been responsible for their rescue?

On an afternoon when the breeze was so trifling that the sails drooped, Captain Whitfield sent word for Manjiro to join him at the midships bulwark to larboard. When Manjiro arrived, Captain Whitfield handed Manjiro his long glass. "Do you see the land?"

"Yes," Manjiro said. Something about the contours of the shoreline looked familiar. He had seen that coastline before. He was looking at his own island! Pain so terrible it took his breath away went through him. He lowered the glass and looked up at Captain Whitfield.

Captain Whitfield shook his head. "No, it is impossible. Even if there were a way ..."

When Captain Whitfield did not continue, Manjiro said, "There will surely be fishing boats out. I am a good swimmer. If you could take the *John Howland* in closer, and lower a boat to take me nearer to Shikoku, I could make it."

"That's doubtful," Captain Whitfield said. "But even

if you could, I would not let you go."

Manjiro handed the spyglass back to Captain Whitfield without looking up at his face. After this he could no longer regard the captain in the same light. He had not asked a great deal. How could Captain Whitfield, who himself was sometimes homesick, deny him the chance to go home? How could he have admired a man with a heart as hard as the rocks on that lonely island where he and his friends had almost perished?

"You don't understand, do you, John? You do not know. My boy, your country has a very old law that anyone who enters a foreign ship—or goes to a foreign country and later returns—will be put to death! Sailing men have known this a long time. Dr. Judd has a copy of the law, given to him by a man who became his beloved friend—a Japanese scholar who escaped but later took his life by his own hand."

Manjiro closed his eyes and rocked back and forth. He saw in his mind the expression on Dr. Judd's face when Fudenojo asked if there were a Dutch ship in the harbor at Honolulu that could take them home. It was true—there must be such a law. That was why the boats, even the lords' boats, were not seaworthy. That was what lay behind the horror stories of what would happen if you went into waters contaminated by barbarians. Feeling as if he were choking, Manjiro said, "Why would they teach me the laws? I am only a fisherman's son, an unworthy . . ."

"Stop that! You are not unworthy. Don't ever let me hear you say it again!"

Captain Whitfield's stern voice so startled Manjiro that he stopped rocking and opened his eyes, but pain and fury still raged inside him.

The captain met his eyes and spoke again, this time gently. "Most everyone is topside," he said.

Manjiro went to the scuttle, slid it open, and went down the companionway to the forecastle living quarters. He opened his sea chest and removed the kimono, now thin and torn, that his mother had made for him. As many times as it had been soaked with seawater, his mother's scent remained. He buried his face in the kimono and wept.

13

Japanese Boy, American Boy

In his diary, Manjiro wrote: *May 7, 1843.*
Today we will enter port at . . . He could not
remember how to make the words. He had to look at
the names Captain Whitfield had printed for him:
Fairhaven, Massachusetts.

Later, he thought he would burst with excitement
when he saw hills rising on the land and, ahead of the
ship, a drawbridge they would pass under.

When they were ready to leave the ship, Manjiro
shook hands with the crew. It made him especially sad

to say good-bye to the men who had rescued him and his friends. "Wipe those tears away," Jake said in a gruff voice. "We'll be sailing together again. Anybody good as you in a blow won't become a landlubber."

Manjiro gave a shaky laugh. What Jake said was true. After that first storm, he had been capable aloft when the weather turned mean. And he had not again gotten sick.

He thanked Mr. Burke for teaching him, and at last stood face to face with Billy. "It is a great sadness to say good-bye," he said.

Billy cleared his throat as if he were going to say something, but only nodded.

"Take care of your—freckles," Manjiro said. When he had asked Captain Whitfield what caused the small brown spots on Billy's face, Captain Whitfield had chuckled and said, "The sun. They're called freckles."

Billy wiped his forefinger under his nose. "I don't reckon we'll be sailing together again. You'll probably become a danged teacher or something."

Manjiro pictured the first time the men of the *John Howland* had killed a whale, how he had earnestly watched so he could teach the people of Tosa how to do it. He had gone without sleep, made himself sick, only to later learn that he would be killed if he returned to his country. Billy, of course, meant that he would probably become a teacher in America. He would have laughed at the thought if tears weren't running down his face. "Good-bye, my friend," he said.

Billy rubbed his finger under his nose again and blinked rapidly. "Take care of yourself, John." He walked quickly away.

Wherever Manjiro went with Captain Whitfield that day, the captain introduced him as "my boy, John."

It pleased Manjiro in one sense and disturbed him in another. He realized that Captain Whitfield had come to look upon him as a son, but while he admired– even loved–Captain Whitfield, he did not think of him as his father. The fisherman buried in Nakanohama, the one he had not said good-bye to, was his father.

The captain didn't take Manjiro to his home. After a few weeks, he left him with a family in Fairhaven and went to New York City.

Five weeks passed before the captain returned–with a bride. "Mrs. Whitfield," Captain Whitfield said, "this is my boy, John."

This Mrs. Whitfield, Manjiro thought, was several years younger than the captain. Her face was not so pretty as some of the American ladies he had seen, but he liked her eyes. They were dark brown, and kind, and they seemed to twinkle with silent merriment.

"Please call me Amelin," she said to Manjiro. Then, glancing up at Captain Whitfield, she said, "You didn't tell me how handsome he is."

Manjiro's face grew warm. He had not minded when his mother's friends said he was handsome. Japanese women loved to tease. But American women were generally more reserved, and he didn't know Mrs. Whitfield. It was embarrassing to hear her say to the captain, and in the hearing of others, that Manjiro was handsome.

Captain and Mrs. Whitfield soon bought a farm on Sconticut Neck, which juts into the sea outside Fairhaven, and began to build a home. At the end of summer, Captain Whitfield enrolled Manjiro in Oxford School, a private school several miles away headed by Miss Allen. After she greeted him, Miss Allen said, "I see that you turned sixteen in June."

Manjiro didn't explain that he had made up the June birthday, nor that in his country he would now be seventeen.

Except for special occasions when he went to Sconticut Neck, he stayed with the captain's sister, who lived near Miss Allen's school.

He did well at school and advanced quickly. Miss Allen frequently invited him to supper. "John," she said to him on one of those occasions, "I know it hurts when some of the other pupils aren't kind to you. I wouldn't worry about it. It's only because you're a good student and they're jealous."

Perhaps some were jealous, Manjiro thought, but there

was another reason some of the students shunned him. When he had asked one of the boys who had at first been friendly if he had done anything to offend, the boy had shaken his head. "It's not that you did anything, it's just that . . . Well, my parents don't want me to get friendly with an Oriental."

"It is enough to have good friends like Job Tripp and Tilley Nelson," Manjiro said now to Miss Allen.

"Job is also an excellent student," Miss Allen said. "Tilley is . . . good-natured."

Manjiro ducked his head so Miss Allen wouldn't see his grin. Tilley was not a very good student, and his pranks tried Miss Allen's patience.

The year turned to 1844; the weather became cold, and snow lay deep on the roads.

Manjiro was glad when spring came and he could again occasionally go home to Sconticut Neck. Except it was not really home. Life here was good, but the pull back to Dai Nippon had not weakened. It was not only the fact that he had not been ready to leave his mother that caused the sorrow that always lay in his heart. Unlike the Americans, who were a mixture of people from many lands, the Nihonjin's ancestry stretched back to the creation of the islands, and traditions handed down through the ages were a part of one's daily life. No amount of love and kindness could make up for such a loss.

Late spring came, school closed for vacation, and

Manjiro went home in great excitement. "Miss Allen says she has taught me all she can!" he told the Whitfields.

Captain Whitfield smiled and nodded. "I know."

"I'm proud of you," Amelin said.

Amelin, Manjiro learned, was very capable. She could cook and sew almost as well as his mother. And when Captain Whitfield was away on business, she helped Mr. O'Brien, whom the captain had hired to take care of the farm. Amelin could wield an ax and tend the crops. She could handle horses as well as Mr. O'Brien—and better than her husband.

Manjiro had his own horse, Hickory. Riding Hickory around the farm, breathing in the sweetness of the apple orchard and the tartness of the alfalfa, he imagined himself the son of a lord in his own country. His land was well tended and yielded fine crops. "You would be proud of me, Okaasan," he murmured.

When he was not working on the farm, Manjiro went down to the wharves. Many times he heard the words "sea fever." Yes, he thought, those were the right words for the reaction to the very smell of the wharves. Sailors did not love the sea. It was not possible to love a place of such vastness, and of such violence. Nor could one hate the sea. Surely nothing could match the sunsets and sunrises, the moon path that made spray look like pearls, or the contentment that came with a gentle breeze.

He kept thinking he might see Billy. Finally he asked questions and learned that Billy had signed on to another ship a few weeks after the *John Howland* had come into port. Evidently the sea was Billy's home. Manjiro hoped Billy had sailed with a good captain. Listening to the sailors, he understood more than ever how fortunate he and his friends were that it had been Captain Whitfield who had rescued them.

Some captains, he learned, were so cruel that they ordered floggings. Captain Whitfield had maintained order with no more than that one shouted word, "Avast!" which meant "Cease!" Nor were all ships clean like the *John Howland*. Some were filthy and rat-infested.

The *John Howland* had gone back out with a different captain, but Manjiro expected that Captain Whitfield was beginning to feel the sea fever too. It would surely not be too long before they sailed. And they would of course go to Honolulu. He would see his Tosa friends.

At the wharves, he also heard arguments about slavery in America. He knew well where Captain Whitfield stood on that subject. The captain hated slavery, and he never hesitated to voice his opinion that people should be judged by their character, not by their color.

Amelin told him that the church they attended was not the church Captain Whitfield had joined as a young man. "The church he loved requires those of color to sit at the back," she said. "So we do not go there." The church Captain Whitfield and Amelin and Manjiro attended let anybody of any color sit wherever they wished to sit.

But both at church and at the wharves, Manjiro saw hatred in some of the strange faces that turned toward him. One evening an old sailor said, "You're one of them slant-eyed Japanee," and spat at Manjiro's feet.

When Manjiro left the wharves, with the hurt still making his chest ache, he thought, Someday I will help the people of my two countries understand each other, and the hating will stop.

14
The Sea Beckons

Each time Captain Whitfield went away on business through the summer, Manjiro thought he would return with the news that they were about to sail. He didn't, and toward the end of summer, the captain smiled broadly and said, "John, you and I have an appointment. I have already talked with the headmaster at Bartlett's Academy—a select school for boys and girls of high intellect with a desire to learn. Mr. Bartlett is particularly impressed with your ability in mathematics. He will accept you as a student."

Manjiro soon found himself poring over books. Sometimes he despaired of ever being ready for the advanced courses that the school offered in surveying and mathematics to those who survived the fall term. But when the year turned to 1845, and the next term came, he was still at the school. He did well in the advanced courses, realized that a knowledge of mathematics would serve him well, and decided to become a navigator.

He saved his allowance until he had enough money to buy a copy of Nathaniel Bowditch's *The New American Practical Navigator*, which was known as the sailor's bible, and studied it far into the night.

"And this Mr. Bowditch's father was a cooper!" Manjiro told Captain Whitfield.

Captain Whitfield frowned. "What are you leading up to, John?"

"Oh, I do not mean to leave Bartlett's Academy, sir. But I saw on the *John Howland* that many of the men have more than one skill. I will be a navigator—*and* a cooper."

Captain Whitfield paced, his hands behind his back. "And you plan to learn this trade from Mr. Hussey?"

Manjiro nodded. "Yes, sir. He and his good wife are going to let me stay with them. I will learn the trade in my spare time."

Captain Whitfield continued to pace, and several times he shook his head.

He is going to forbid me to do this thing I want very much to do, Manjiro thought.

When he at last spoke, though, Captain Whitfield said only, "I must go away on business. But Mrs. Whitfield will be here."

Early in his apprenticeship, Manjiro understood Captain Whitfield's negative attitude about Mr. Hussey's trade school. The captain either knew or suspected what Manjiro had not suspected. Mr. and Mrs. Hussey seemed not to understand that the young apprentices needed nourishment. When Manjiro was trying to do his homework for Bartlett's in the evenings, after he had put in the necessary time for learning to make barrels, he found himself thinking of food instead. For breakfast and supper, Mrs. Hussey served the apprentices only bread. For the noon meal, they received a plate of dumplings.

He was always tired now, and sometimes his mind wandered. He had only a few weeks left of the apprenticeship, and was still managing to maintain his grades at Bartlett's, the day he collapsed.

15
An Opportunity

E at your chicken soup," Amelin said.

"I'm fine now," Manjiro said. "It's time I got up."

"So get up—and have a relapse." Amelin, plump with child, sat down on the side of the bed. "You're so close to finishing . . . You do want to finish the apprenticeship, don't you, John? And you must graduate from Bartlett's. It would break the captain's heart if you didn't do that. You need your strength back before you get out of bed."

"You are as strict a nurse as my mother." Mentioning his mother brought tears to Manjiro's eyes. He turned his face away from Amelin.

"It's all right to cry, John," Amelin said. "It's also a sign that you're still sick."

When he was well, he finished the apprenticeship. The day he graduated from Bartlett's Academy, shortly before his eighteenth birthday in June of 1845, Captain Whitfield was there. Beaming proudly, he put his arm across Manjiro's shoulders. "I wouldn't have missed this for the world, John. Amelin would have liked to come, but she's too far advanced to go out in public."

During the ride home in the buggy, Manjiro sensed that Captain Whitfield was excited about something. His own excitement grew. The captain's business trip must have concerned a whaling voyage. He and Captain Whitfield were going back to sea!

Some of Manjiro's friends were there when he walked into the house on Sconticut Neck. Amelin had made a cake for him, and she laughed brightly and hugged him and said how proud she was. Behind her smiles, Manjiro sensed a sadness. When he had an opportunity, he whispered, "What is the name of the ship?"

"Shh," she said. "He'll tell you."

When the guests had gone, Captain Whitfield said, "John, I am going to make a whaling trip on the *William Eliza* as soon as I can get a crew together."

Manjiro's pulse quickened.

"You will not be part of the crew."

It took Manjiro a moment to accept that he had heard correctly. Fearing that his hurt and anger might show in his eyes, he looked down at the floor.

"Mrs. Whitfield needs you here—as do I," Captain Whitfield said. "Mr. O'Brien will continue to do most of the work, but you will be in charge of the farm."

"It—it is a great honor." Manjiro lifted his head, but he still did not look into Captain Whitfield's face. He liked the farm, but he yearned to go back to sea. And now, because of his studies, he could do much more than clean decks and reef sails. Captain Whitfield knew that, and surely knew how much he wanted to see his friends in Honolulu. Why was the captain doing this to him?

After Captain Whitfield sailed, and his aunt came to stay until the baby was born, Amelin said, "John, he fears that if you leave, you will not come back to us. You know, don't you, that you are a son to him."

"And he is like a father to me," Manjiro said. "But . . ."

"But he is not your father. And you miss Fudenojo and the others." She gave him a straight look. "And you dream that they have found a way for all of you to return to Japan."

"Yes," Manjiro murmured.

With the birth of William Henry, though, he found himself feeling responsible for the new baby, and thinking less and less about leaving.

His love deepened as William Henry crawled, then took toddling steps into his arms. And there was always work to do on the farm. Mr. O'Brien praised him for jobs well done and told him he had a knack for farming. They would have a good yield of potatoes and apples, and more hay than they needed.

The faces of Fudenojo and the others dimmed, and he thought less often about his family.

But when Ira Davis, now a captain, came to the Whitfields' home and asked Manjiro to sail with him as navigator on a whaling voyage, Manjiro's hope and excitement surged again. Not only would he be the navigator, he would sail with a man he knew from the *John Howland*, a man Captain Whitfield knew well. Captain Davis had been first a greenhand on one of Captain Whitfield's ships, and then a harpooneer on the *John Howland* when Manjiro was aboard. Manjiro had not become friends with Ira Davis, but he respected his ability, and admired his ambition and determination.

A thin-faced man with a well-trimmed beard, Captain Davis laced his fingers together and circled his thumbs around each other as he talked. "The name of my ship is the *Franklin*," he said. "She's a hundred feet long—273 tons. And I'll have a twenty-four-man crew."

Manjiro thought about the way Captain Whitfield said "we," not "I," to make all on board feel that it was their ship, too. But the worst thing he knew, or had ever heard, about Captain Davis was that he brooded at times, and had a nervous disposition.

Manjiro didn't let Captain Davis see his excitement. All he said was, "Thank you for asking me, sir. I will think about it."

"Isaachar Aiken will be my chief mate," Captain Davis said.

It had been Mr. Aiken, a quiet, capable man, who had treated Juusuke's foot. Manjiro liked Mr. Aiken and had great respect for him.

Captain Davis stopped circling his thumbs and smoothed his beard. "You might also be interested to know that fishing boats are venturing farther from your country's shores. Apparently there is great discontent in your country. And we've been able to put in at one of the Loochoos for a short time. I'm told that an American ship managed to trade a bolt of material for some chickens and vegetables."

Captain Davis cleared his throat. "And considering you're, ah, like them, speak the language and all, I expect you can do better."

It took control for Manjiro to keep a straight face. To Americans, all Orientals looked alike and spoke the same language. But although that was incorrect, Captain Davis had made the right point.

"You know how desperately we need a supply station in that area," Captain Davis said.

Manjiro had learned about the Loochoos at Bartlett's Academy and from listening to the talk at the wharves. They were a chain of small islands between southern Kyushu, a large Japanese island, and Taiwan, a Chinese island. Okinawa was the largest of the islands, which were also called the Ryukyus. They were under the dominion of China, but the real rule was Japanese.

Captain Davis stood up. "We'll be sailing into the Japan Sea. And I failed to mention that you will be the second mate."

Being the second mate, whose role made him popular with neither captain nor crew, was not a job he relished, Manjiro thought. But he could abide it for the sizable share of the profits the second mate received. And as navigator, he would have the opportunity to apply what he had learned. But Captain Davis's statement, "You know how desperately we need a supply station in that area," was the crowning argument. Manjiro would stand a better chance of opening one than a white man. This was his opportunity to do something for Captain Whitfield. To do something for all American sailing men.

He couldn't accept Captain Davis's offer now, though. He wanted to talk to Amelin first. It would be better to go with her blessing, since in Captain Whitfield's absence, she spoke for him.

After Captain Davis took his leave, Manjiro went in

search of Amelin. He found her in the small, sunlit room where she sewed while William Henry played. His heart twisted when he saw William Henry lying on a pallet, sound asleep

"Tell me, John," Amelin said in a low voice.

Knowing that quiet talk did not disturb William Henry, Manjiro sat down on the settee and told Amelin about Captain Davis's offer.

"Of course you must go," Amelin said. "It's what you have prepared yourself to do."

"Captain Whitfield might be angry with me. He charged me to take care of the farm and you and William Henry." He felt foolish saying it. Mr. O'Brien took care of the farm—under Amelin's supervision. And Amelin didn't need anybody to take care of her.

Rethreading her needle, Amelin said, "Captain Whitfield would go if he were in your shoes. Yes, he may be angry at first, but he will also be proud of you."

Manjiro stood. "Thank you, Amelin," he said, and heard the catch in his voice when he added, "Most of all I wish Captain Whitfield to be proud of me."

That night, he wrote in his diary,

March 9, 1846

It is great sadness to leave Amelin and William H. and may not see again. But what I hope to do is for benefit of all.

Manjiro went into Fairhaven and told Captain Davis he would be pleased to go as the navigator on the *Franklin*. Then he sought out a seamstress. Nervous about entering the establishment, he relaxed somewhat when a large, motherly-looking woman approached him. When he told her he wanted her to make a kimono, she smiled warmly and showed him materials.

He selected a colorful, rich-looking cloth and sketched what he wanted—a kimono that came to the knees—like the ones some of the samurai wore. He would look handsome in such a kimono, and he would command respect from the Loochoo people. "I am a poor artist," he said with a small laugh. "Can you make?"

"Of course," she said. "She's going to love it. Now you must tell me about her, since I gather this is a surprise. Is she shorter than I?" She laughed. "She's slimmer, I'm sure. Her arms—it's important to know about how long her arms are."

Manjiro's face had become hot. "She . . . She is about my size," he said.

When the seamstress had taken measurements, he fled from the shop. But a bit later, he laughed aloud. She would naturally not understand that the kimono was for a man—for himself. American men wore dark, sedate clothes like those he was wearing now.

16

A Disappointment

An early summer sun warmed the deck. The sails caught the wind; Manjiro watched the land fall away. The *Franklin* was a sturdy ship, and there were skilled and seasoned men aboard. But half of the crew were greenhands still in their mid-teens.

As the months passed, he could see the young men toughen and become more capable. Most of them would make good sailors.

When the ship entered port at Guam in March of 1847, he wrote to Captain Whitfield, apologized for leaving, and explained his hopes to open a trading port in the Loochoos. He now knew it would not be an easy matter. Men from another ship had told him they put in at a Loochoo island and sent a boat ashore to see if they could trade for food. An official on the island refused to trade with them and said if they were not gone in two days, he would cut their mooring lines.

It would be different when he went ashore, Manjiro told himself. He would point out that despite China and Japan's power in the Loochoos, the islands had their own king. He would make them understand that it would just be a matter of trading fresh meat and produce for items the islanders needed, and that this surely posed no threat.

When they were again at sea, he told Captain Davis of his plan to open a trading post on one of the islands.

"From what I've heard of late, there's not much chance," Captain Davis said. He walked away muttering under his breath.

Watching him go, Manjiro frowned. Something was happening to Captain Davis. The other men were aware of it, too. Big Jim, the blacksmith, had pointedly said, "We best keep a close eye on him. More'n one man's gone mad at sea. I was on a whaler where the cook went berserk and kilt two men with a meat cleaver before we could get irons on him."

The *Franklin* caught whales in the South China Sea, sailed past Taiwan, and anchored off the coast of a tiny

Loochoo island to try to trade. Captain Davis had brought along a dozen bolts of cloth. He decided that he and Manjiro and the two men accompanying them should take four bolts to the small island.

When they reached the island, Manjiro found that he could not understand what the islanders said, and they only shook their heads when he spoke to them. He believed their language came from a mixture of Chinese and Japanese, changed over time to one peculiarly their own. He also realized that he had a problem when it came to speaking in his native tongue. He no longer thought in Japanese. But with hand language and a basic understanding of the tact and patience that were a part of Oriental bargaining, he managed to trade the four bolts of cloth for two cows.

Manjiro was jubilant. This was not the place to open a trading post—but they *had* traded. He expected Captain Davis to be pleased. Instead, he was angry. "They got the best of the bargain," he said. "The cows are old. The meat will be too tough to eat!" He narrowed his eyes. "You people stick together, don't you?"

When they stopped at a larger island a few weeks later to try again to trade, Captain Davis said to Manjiro, "You sir, will not go with us this time. I know what you're up to!"

Captain Davis and the others came back with the bolts of cloth.

Sailing about 160 miles off the Japanese coast, the

Franklin took a northeasterly course up the Pacific. At one place off the southeastern coast of Honshu, bonito swarmed, and sails were furled so the crew could fish.

In the distance, Manjiro spotted a small island. He put his spyglass to his eye and swayed with the jolt of what he saw. He knew that island; he knew it all too well. For long minutes he studied the island, and decided no one was there—except three who lay beneath stones. He lowered the glass and stood remembering, seeing it all again—the raw albatross, the cave, scraping the salt off seaweed, Fudenojo falling on the rocks ...

Boats, many small boats, were approaching. The fishermen were Nihonjin! Captain Davis had been right about their coming farther out.

The boats—perhaps twenty of them—were more seaworthy than the one in which he and his friends had been caught in the storm. The fishermen did not seem to be afraid; they were coming closer to the *Franklin*. Something was obviously happening inside Japan. Commoners were rebelling—quietly perhaps, but rebelling nevertheless.

Watching the boats approach, Manjiro murmured, "This is my chance."

Captain Davis had shut himself up in his cabin. Nowadays, the captain looked around at the men with fear in his eyes, then went to his cabin and stayed for hours.

Manjiro went to his quarters, removed his jacket and put on the kimono, then went back up the companionway and across the deck to the bulwark. The yardarms rocked gently, the creaking was soft and rhythmic. The men were quiet, smiling and encouraging him with the thumbs-up sign.

When the boats were close enough, he called a greeting, then asked the fishermen where they were from, what their province was. *"Anata no okuni wa? Doko desuka?"*

The men stared blankly up at him.

"Lower a boat for me, please." He had forgotten how much Nihonjin depended on facial expression and body language. He needed to be close to them.

He climbed down into the boat; he and Paddy McNulty rowed slowly until they were face to face with the fishermen. Again Manjiro asked which was their province.

The men shrugged and shook their heads.

"Watashi wa Tosa no Shikoku kara kimashita," Manjiro said. (I am from Tosa ... Shikoku.)

"Sendai," one of the men said. He continued to talk rapidly, and others joined in.

Hopelessly, Manjiro shook his head. Their dialect was different from that spoken in Tosa. While he tried to get one word, the fishermen were many words beyond. All he really understood was that they were from "Sendai." Was Sendai a province, or a town?

"Sendai," he said and, with signs as well as words, asked if they would take him with them.

The fishermen became alarmed and started moving away.

When Paddy dipped his oars to follow them, Manjiro shook his head. "It is no use." He felt like crying, but he could not cry in front of a member of the crew.

17
Reunion in Honolulu

W hen the *Franklin* entered port at Honolulu in October 1848, Manjiro immediately went to see Dr. Judd. After they exchanged greetings and talk about the *Franklin*'s voyage, Dr. Judd said, "Captain Whitfield looked fit when he was in Honolulu eleven months ago."

"I am pleased to hear that," Manjiro said. "I know he will be happy when he can go home and see his William Henry. He is a smart child, and everything is funny to him."

Dr. Judd smiled and nodded.

"Dr. Judd," Manjiro said then, "I am most anxious to see my friends. Can you tell me where to find them?"

After a moment's hesitation, Dr. Judd said, "I know only where you can find Toraemon." Explaining as he drew, he sketched a map, then said, "I recall that I was no more than courteous when you and the others first came to Honolulu. I apologize. It was not really you five with whom I was upset."

Manjiro nodded. "Captain Whitfield told me about your friend who escaped from Japan—then took his life. I expect he believed he had dishonored his family."

"Including his ancestors," Dr. Judd said. "And he felt that he had offended the soul of Japan." He shrugged. "I didn't understand then, and I don't now. Nor do I understand Japan's isolationist attitude."

His expression softened and his eyes became sad; he looked at Manjiro as if he were about to tell him something. Manjiro could see him change his mind. All he said was, "Please give Toraemon my regards."

Toraemon lived outside Honolulu and worked as a carpenter's apprentice. When Manjiro arrived at the small house, the two men hugged and laughed and wept.

Where are the others? Manjiro wondered. Something was wrong.

"Sit and rest," Toraemon said. "I will make tea."

Toraemon spoke in the Tosa dialect, and it sounded good to Manjiro's ears. Gently, he said, "Tell me. And speak slowly, Toraemon."

Toraemon's face crumpled. "Juusuke is dead."

Manjiro felt more than heard the cry that came from somewhere inside him.

"It was the old wound to his foot. It became very bad and poisoned his body," Toraemon said. "The generous people of Honolulu—indeed, the people of all the island of Oahu, including the queen herself—spared no expense. He received the best of treatment. But I do not know whether he wanted to live longer. Always he suffered. And always he was homesick. His last words were, 'I may die here, but my spirit will go back to my own country.'"

Toraemon picked up a piece of wood from which the figure of a duck—no, a goose—was emerging, and started carving. "It's a *nene*, a Hawaiian goose." After a pause, he said, "Fudenojo has changed his name to Denzo."

Manjiro nodded. It was not unusual for Nihonjin to change their names, sometimes for easier pronunciation, sometimes because they simply liked another name better. But since Manjiro had not been here to make a gradual adjustment to the new name, his friend would always be Fudenojo to him.

"Denzo and Goemon are not here," Toraemon said.

Questions rushed into Manjiro's mind, but he kept his

silence. He must let Toraemon tell him in his own way.

Toraemon blew wood dust off his carving. "They had no reason to be discontent here. Dr. Judd gave them work in his home until they found better opportunities. We will get back to that. Now I will tell you how it came about that Denzo and Goemon left.

"A Mr. Cox, captain of the *Colorado*, a merchant ship, was en route to China. That was last November—almost a year ago. Captain Whitfield was here at the time. It turned out that Captain Whitfield knew this Captain Cox. And Captain Whitfield knew how much we wanted to go home."

Manjiro drew in his breath. Fudenojo and Goemon had gone home! But Toraemon had not gone with them. And there had been an almost imperceptible pause, a slight change of expression, when he reached the *we* in his last statement.

Toraemon put his carving down and continued to talk while he made the tea. "Captain Whitfield spoke with Captain Cox, and Cox agreed to let Denzo and Goemon work their passage on the *Colorado*. Captain Whitfield bought suits and shoes for them. He gave them all the silver he could spare. Dr. Judd and Chaplain Damon and others gave them farewell gifts." Toraemon hesitated again. "There has been no word of them since."

Bringing the tea and coconut cookies, he added, "I didn't trust that Captain Cox. I had heard that he was a

dog. I told Goemon and Denzo that the man was only using them. That they would have to work like devils for their passage."

Sweet-scented air and muted music floated through the open windows. "But Captain Whitfield made arrangements for them to go?" Manjiro asked. Captain Whitfield would not make arrangements for Fudenojo and Goemon to sail with a captain who was a dog.

"*Hai.*" (Yes.) "This Captain Cox promised Captain Whitfield to look after them."

After a moment, Manjiro said, "You like carpentry work."

"*Hai.* I like it."

And Toraemon had been drawn to this island from the start, Manjiro remembered. But how could it be that Toraemon did not want to return home? Maybe he was wrong; maybe Toraemon truly had some good reason for not trusting Captain Cox.

"I was surprised that Goemon went," Toraemon said. "He had been seeing a Christian girl." He hesitated, then added, "He has converted to the Christian religion."

Manjiro started to tell Toraemon about the church he went to in Fairhaven, about his belief that God had created all and therefore cared about all. He changed his mind; it might start a discussion that led to disagreement. He only nodded.

"Let us not talk any more tonight," Toraemon said.

"Tomorrow we will talk—and I will introduce you to some of my friends."

Manjiro had been with Toraemon for twenty days when the carpenter he worked for came hurrying from the town. "I have just seen a sailor who was on board the *Colorado*," he said. "It is in port. The sailor said Denzo and Goemon are still aboard!"

Manjiro and Toraemon rushed to the harbor. It was true. Fudenojo and Goemon, exhausted and sad, were back.

When they had eaten and rested, they told their story. After several months at sea, Captain Cox had gone ashore with them on what he considered a safe stretch of Japan's northernmost island, Yezo (Hokkaido).

"There was only one house in sight," Fudenojo said. "After calling and calling, we went inside. They had left all their belongings, even their sandals and raincoats. It was obvious that they had spotted the ship and seen us coming—and fled."

Goemon picked up the story. "We spent all night sitting on a hillside. Captain Cox stayed with us. We knew there must be other houses farther inland. We built a fire both to keep us warm and so the people could see us on the hillside. But no one came."

Fudenojo told how Captain Cox had refused to

leave them in such a lonely, desolate place, reminded them that he had promised Captain Whitfield to look after them.

"He probably picked out a lonely, desolate island to take you ashore," Toraemon said. "He didn't want to lose two good—unpaid—hands for the rest of his trip."

"You do him an injustice, I think," Fudenojo said quietly.

That night, Manjiro dreamed that he was in the water, swimming, fighting the waves. He could see the rocky shore of Shikoku. But although he swam and swam, he could not reach the shore. His own voice, calling out for someone to help him get home, awakened him. "I'm sorry," he said when he realized that he had also awakened Fudenojo. He did not explain that seeing his friends had made him almost unbearably homesick and had brought on the dream.

During his stay in Hawaii, Manjiro talked with many people. Among them was the Reverend Samuel C. Damon, the seaman's chaplain and editor of *The Friend*, a newspaper devoted to sailing men and their ships.

"A letter from Captain Whitfield, who is still at sea, has just arrived," Chaplain Damon said.

Fearing that Captain Whitfield's letter would say he never wanted to see him again, Manjiro nervously opened the envelope.

As he read, he relaxed. The captain's letter was

warm. Amelin had written to him that she had "encouraged John to accept Captain Davis's offer." The captain wrote that he realized that he had not wanted to accept that his son was a man grown, a man who had to make his own decisions. Manjiro lingered over the line, "I am proud of you, John."

The letter also passed on Amelin's report about William Henry—the clever things he said. Then the captain told about his own whaling trip, how many barrels of oil they had, and said that he might have to cut the trip short because his ship was leaky.

When he had read the letter for the third time, Manjiro wrote to Captain Whitfield and told about Fudenojo and Goemon's return. He wrote how much he missed William Henry, then went into some detail about his hope to open a trading post on one of the Loochoo islands.

"I will see that he receives it," Chaplain Damon said. He agreed that a supply post on one of the Ryukyu islands was much needed. "I think you set yourself a difficult, if not impossible task, John," he said. "But I will help in any way I can. When you're ready, we'll ask through *The Friend* for donations of equipment you'll need."

"America has done much for me," Manjiro said. "This supply post will be my gift to America."

He also talked with officers from English ships, and to officers from other countries who could speak

English. That included conversation with a Dutch officer who was a little drunk. "My countrymen on Deshima have Japanese servants, you know," the Dutch officer said. "Of course, the servants mock my countrymen. They think we Dutch are stupid clowns."

"Your countrymen are far from stupid," Manjiro said. "It is the Japanese government that is stupid."

"Well, well," the Dutch officer said. "Here is a Nippon who has seen the light."

With prompting, the Dutchman told all he knew about what was going on inside Japan.

When Manjiro put together the information he had gathered from various sources, he knew beyond doubt that there was much disquiet in Japan.

For a long time, the lower classes had staged uprisings that had been brutally crushed, but now a great scholar had been imprisoned because he had openly criticized Japan's system. A popular poet had been executed because his work spoke against the isolation policy. But the dissenting voices were not silenced, and the uprisings were becoming stronger.

There was, as well, increased murmuring against the Bakufu—the Tokugawa Shogunate—for its treatment of the emperor. For more than two hundred years, the shoguns had kept the emperors in impoverished seclusion at Kyoto. And now, Manjiro concluded, people in high places wanted the circumstances befitting their emperor restored to him.

When he had learned all he could, and the time for the *Franklin* to sail drew near, he talked to his friends about their return to Japan. "I know the mistakes we have made," he said. "And I know what we must do."

Toraemon picked up the carving and his blade. Fudenojo and Goemon looked at Manjiro.

Although he was the navigator for a ship and gave orders to men twice his age, it took him aback for a second that Fudenojo looked to him with submissive confidence.

"When the time comes, we must go to a well-populated Loochoo island," Manjiro said. "And we must go in style, with a good whaling boat—and items that will intrigue the lords."

Goemon gasped. "The lords!"

"*Hai,*" Manjiro said. "If we are fortunate, we will quietly work with the port people to set up a trading post. In time we will blend into the citizenry and be able to go home. But we must consider the possibility that we will be arrested. If we are, we want to appear worthy of being turned over to high officials of Dai Nippon. It is they who are most likely to be curious about other parts of the world. And every day we stay alive will improve our chances."

"You will be in the greatest danger," Toraemon said. "You went to America of your own free will."

"The rest of us couldn't help it if the ship that rescued us brought us here," Goemon said.

"*Hai,*" Manjiro said again. He did not explain that he believed his having lived in America was actually their key to survival if they were arrested. His countrymen were curious about America. That was why the fishermen had approached the *Franklin*. American ships—and the people who manned them—intrigued the Japanese. And if fishermen were curious, the lords would be much more so. They would want to know everything about the country at the feet of the world.

18
A Captain Gone Mad

It was now March of 1849, and in the four months since they had left Honolulu, Captain Davis's condition had grown steadily worse. Manjiro had never been more exhausted.

Wearily he went down the foredeck companionway and to his quarters. He removed his outer clothing and his shoes and socks, then stretched out on his bunk and went back over the past four months.

After whaling for a time, they had gone to Guam, where he and Isaachar Aiken had asked for medical

help for the captain. But when they described his symptoms to the doctor, he shook his head. "He needs to be in a hospital," the doctor said, "and there are no hospitals on Guam. There is one in Manila."

And so they were bound for Manila, in the Luzons. Manjiro and Isaachar Aiken worked in twelve-hour shifts so that one of them would always be on deck. Fortunately, Captain Davis spent much of the time in his cabin. When he paced the quarterdeck, one could tell that he was listening to voices in his head, and sometimes he flew into nonsensical rages, accusing men of spying on him or stealing from his cabin.

There was much tension—flaring tempers and grumbling. Some of the veteran whalers, led by Big Jim, had asked for a meeting with Chief Aiken and Manjiro, and told them they were in favor of putting Captain Davis in irons.

Manjiro put his arm over his eyes. He and Isaachar were faced with an awesome dilemma. The men were close to rebellion, but the captain of a ship was like the head of a country. To take command away from him could lead to imprisonment—or hanging.

A tap sounded on the door, and Manjiro thought, Go away. Let me rest. Aloud he said, "Enter."

The cook's helper, a boy named Grant, pushed the door open. Manjiro swung his legs over the side of the bed. Something was wrong. The boy was pale, his eyes round with fear.

"It's the captain, sir," the boy said. "I was going out on the fo'c'sle and I seen ... He, Captain Davis, has a pistol in one hand and a harpoon in the other. He's saying they mean to kill him, but he'll get some of them first."

"Where is he?"

"He's backed up against the fo'c'sle bulwarks close to where the anchors be, so there's no way to jump him from behind. It's awful, sir ..."

"Who's there?"

"Mr. Wang ..."

The old Chinese sailmaker. No help.

"...and Steve Rosset, Mr. Aiken, and Big Jim ..."

Big Jim. Good. "The scuttle slide? Is it open?"

"Yes, sir. When I seen what was happening, I was in such a hurry to get back down, I ..."

"Stay here," Manjiro said.

Barefoot he ran, on through the scullery, then up the forecastle companionway. Silently he slipped out onto the deck, praying that Big Jim and the other men would know he was there but would not give away his presence.

His voice wouldn't sound like Captain Whitfield's, but he knew the words and the tone—and every man who had ever sailed with Captain Whitfield responded to them. His mouth was dry; the horrifying thought went through his mind that his voice would come out no louder than a squeak. He moistened his lips, swallowed, then shouted, "Avast, Ira Davis!"

Captain Davis jerked his head around; Big Jim leaped, grabbed the captain's right arm, and pushed it upward. The sound of the shot echoed as half a dozen other men rushed the captain and wrestled the harpoon away from him.

Manjiro stood trembling, and when the men had Captain Davis in irons, he went back to his quarters and cried.

19
A Loss

anjiro soaked up the July warmth, the sea's calm rhythm, and the relaxed atmosphere. "After what we been through, we deserve this," Big Jim had said, and Manjiro agreed.

Before they had reached Manila, they had coped with one more nightmare—what one of the men described as "the worst typhoon I ever had the displeasure of dancing with."

Once they had made port and taken Captain Davis to the hospital, the crew had been eager to repair the storm damage and get back to sea. Although he, too, had not wanted to linger, Manjiro had enjoyed the respite and had made a purchase while the *Franklin* was in port. He had bought a parrot for William Henry. Imagining William Henry's face when he saw the parrot, Manjiro laughed to himself.

"Sail ho! Starboard of the bow," came a call from a man perched on a foremast yard.

Along with Captain Aiken, Manjiro watched the ship approach. He put the spyglass to his eye. "It is Captain Woodard of New Bedford! He is a friend of Captain Whitfield's."

"Then it's you he wants to see," Captain Aiken said. "When we speak her, go over and make the gam with him, and I'll stay on board."

"Thank you," Manjiro said. According to protocol, the captains visited on one ship and the officers on the other.

When Manjiro stood on the quarterdeck with Captain Woodard, the captain said, "I had hoped we'd meet."

The expression on Captain Woodard's craggy face alarmed Manjiro. "You have news of Captain Whitfield?"

"Aye, I do. His ship was leaky and he had to come home."

Manjiro blew out a relieved breath. It was bad to have a leaky ship and have to return home before you filled enough barrels, but he had thought it might be even worse news. "And how are Amelin and my William Henry? He is a big boy now, I am sure." Manjiro laughed. "In Guam, I bought for him a beautiful parrot. Already the parrot can say 'hello,' and I will teach it many more words before we reach home port."

"John," Captain Woodard said, "I don't know how to soften this. William Henry died of pneumonia back in the winter."

The *Franklin* at last arrived home in August 1849. Manjiro stood on the quarterdeck as the helmsman maneuvered the ship into port. How good it was to be back in Fairhaven. But his heart was heavy, and he felt older than his twenty-two years. He could not even smile, much less dance and cheer like the other men.

For a few minutes after the men had walked onto shore, he stood watching the joyful, tearful reunions. He pictured William Henry as he would have looked now, a four-year-old with a bright inquisitive face and a smile that would move the most jaded heart.

He turned away, helped Captain Aiken with the final details, then hefted his sea chest onto his shoulder.

He had just stepped onto the ground when he saw Captain Whitfield coming toward him. Manjiro put the chest down. For a moment, they stood looking at each other. Then Captain Whitfield came forward and folded his arms around Manjiro.

When they were on the way home in the carriage, Captain Whitfield said, "John, the letter you sent after Captain Woodard told you about William Henry's death was a great comfort to Amelin and me. We read it over and over. Your love for William Henry, and for us, helped more than you can know."

They rode in silence for a time. Manjiro listened to the clop-clop of the horses' hooves, filled his eyes with the beauty of trees.

"I was sorry to hear about Ira Davis," Captain Whitfield said at last.

"It was very bad," Manjiro said.

"But let us get on to more pleasant things. John, I'm very proud of you. I understand that when the crew voted for a new captain, you lost by only two votes."

Manjiro squirmed. "Yes, I was most surprised." That was an understatement. When his name had been, as the men termed it, "put in the hat," he had been embarrassed. It seemed to him that Isaachar Aiken would automatically take over as captain. But even Isaachar had said no, that it was not done that way, that the men voted.

"But becoming the chief mate was not at all bad," Captain Whitfield said. "Am I right so far?"

Manjiro laughed. "Whaling men are good mail service."

The horses moved along at an easy gait. Manjiro

thought Captain Whitfield was as pleased as he to have this time when there were just the two of them. Those times had been few from the day Captain Whitfield had rescued him and his friends.

"I also heard about the storm that hit you before you reached Manila," Captain Whitfield said.

"It was a bad one. The worst I have ever been in."

"And had it not been for your superior navigation, I am told, the *Franklin* might not have made it."

Manjiro realized that his palms were sweating.

"You've had nightmares about it?" Captain Whitfield asked.

Manjiro hesitated. Thinking they were a weakness in him, he had told no one about the nightmares. There was always fear of the storm itself, but he had not panicked since that time when he climbed with Jake. It was after the typhoon, when the crew cheered him, that he had begun to shake.

'The nightmares," he said, "are most strange. I am making mistakes. I cannot do anything right. And all are going to die because of me. But when the storm was actually happening, I did not have such thoughts."

Sitting at ease with the reins loose in his hands, the captain glanced over at him. "They were there," he said. "You were just too busy to notice them. That's why they came out later in the form of nightmares."

Speaking of the typhoon and the nightmares had relieved a tension inside Manjiro. He leaned forward.

The rich late-summer smell of the farm saturated the air; they were almost there. "How is Hickory?"

"Hickory's gotten fat and lazy. He needs exercise. John, Amelin has a quiet dinner planned for you this weekend. I understand that a certain young lady—Nell Adams—will be among the guests. She has not married—and she's very pretty."

Amelin was behind the matchmaking, Manjiro thought, but Captain Whitfield was also promoting it. He and Nell had enjoyed some good discussions when they went to Bartlett's Academy. They had even exchanged a few kisses. But he would have no time for such friendships now. He already knew what he was going to do after his visit with Captain Whitfield and Amelin.

"Tonight," Manjiro said, "there will just be we . . . three." His voice broke.

A shadow crossed Captain Whitfield's face. "John, you were there when William Henry was born," he said. "I was there when he died. In his short time on this earth he was loved by a wonderful woman—and two good men."

For a while, Manjiro thought, those two men and the wonderful woman would sit and talk and console each other. But it would not be for very long. Every whaler on the sea knew that California had won independence from Mexico and was occupied by United States forces—and that its mountains were heavy with gold.

Manjiro's part of the profits from the *Franklin*'s trip would come to more than $350. That was a lot of money, but it was not enough to take Fudenojo, Goemon, Toraemon, and him to a Loochoo island in style.

20
A Plan

The sky turned a deeper blue, and the early morning chill foretold the coming of autumn. Manjiro had been home a month now. He had been pleased to find that Tilley Nelson, his friend from their days at Miss Allen's school, was still in Fairhaven. "Tilley," he said, "would you consider going with me to California to search for gold?"

"Can you wait until tomorrow?" Tilley said. "I need to mend my other pair of pants."

Manjiro laughed. Tilley had not changed.

When Manjiro spoke to Captain Whitfield about his plan to search for gold, the captain's reaction surprised him. He had expected Captain Whitfield to try to talk him out of going. Stories circulated about the dangers of searching for gold. But far from trying to get him to reconsider, the captain tapped the table with his fist, and his eyes shone. "How I envy you," he said. "It will be a great adventure, John."

In a canvas bag, Manjiro packed along with clothing his copy of Bowditch's *New American Practical Navigator*, his biography of George Washington, a nautical almanac, a map of the United States, and some navigation instruments. When he said good-bye to Captain Whitfield and Amelin, he looked at them until Amelin said with a laugh that he seemed to be memorizing their faces.

Manjiro and Tilley left on a crisp, sunlit day in late October 1849. They worked their passage on a lumber ship and finally arrived in San Francisco at the end of May 1850. From San Francisco they took a paddle steamer to Sacramento. There they joined a mule train taking men and supplies to a gold-mining settlement up in the Sierra Nevadas.

On the second day of the trip, an icy rain fell. When they finally arrived in the town, they were wet, exhausted, and chilled through.

"I sort of like you fellers," the mule train leader said, "so I aim to pass on a word of advice. I noticed you ain't wearing weapons. Keep it that way. You'll live longer."

"Thank you, Mr. Riggs," Manjiro said. He had told Tilley the same thing—that wearing a gun was like a dare some men couldn't pass up. Tilley had been unconvinced.

"I guess that goes for knives too," Tilley said to Manjiro, and gave an exaggerated sigh.

Without bothering to look anywhere else, they took a room in the boardinghouse Mr. Riggs had recommended. The small room had two hard single beds, a washbasin and pitcher, and a rickety dresser.

"Home, sweet home," Tilley said.

Rubbing his backside, Manjiro said, "Do not be so cheerful, please. It may be as Mr. Riggs said, that mules are more surefooted and smarter than horses, but I prefer riding Hickory—with a saddle."

When they had changed to dry clothes, they went across the muddy street to a café to eat supper. Tilley took a bite of the boiled beef and mashed potatoes, and made a face. "They have a nerve to charge fifty cents for this stuff."

Compared to raw albatross, it was quite good, Manjiro thought. Chewing on a piece of the meat, he glanced around. Perhaps a dozen people, some of whom spoke in foreign languages he had never heard, were eating. A few men stood at the bar. Women with piled-up curls and low-cut dresses made open advances to them. Other men played cards at tables, their whiskey glasses at their fingertips.

He took a swallow of his tepid, bitter coffee. Most of the people in here had either not heard or had failed to heed Mr. Riggs's advice. Some of the guns and knives were concealed, but only a greenhorn sailor would be unable to spot them.

Tilley leaned across the table, his eyes glittering. "But other than the food, it's exciting, isn't it?"

For a moment, it took Manjiro aback. Sometimes, it was hard to remember that he and Tilley were the same age—twenty-three. He didn't want to act as if he knew everything, which he was inclined to do, but Tilley's naïveté could get them in trouble. "No," he finally said. "It is not exciting. It is sad. We must stay clear of the gamblers—and the women. And we must say little. We do not want to draw attention to ourselves. I feel much anger and suspicion here."

He had no sooner said it than two men at the bar began to quarrel, one accusing the other of stealing some of his gold dust. The one who made the accusation was a burly, muscular man with an Irish brogue. The one he accused of stealing the dust was a wiry old man. No, Manjiro decided, he was not old—probably under forty. The man's weathered face and whisker stubble only made him look old.

"I do not take kindly to being called a thief," the older man drawled.

"That old guy's crazy to argue with the big Irisher," Tilley said in a low voice. "He'll get himself murdered."

"I do not think so," Manjiro said.

"Ye're a thief!" the big man yelled. "An egg-sucking, lily-livered . . ."

Like a bullet, the older man's left fist slammed upward into the Irishman's stomach, and as the Irishman bent over, the older man clipped his neck with the side of his palm. The Irishman went down on his hands and knees.

The cardplayers had scarcely looked up; the women who had turned to watch the short-lived fight began flirting again.

Manjiro looked over at Tilley, whose mouth was hanging open.

"Since the Irishman accused the older man of stealing gold dust from him, they are probably partners," Manjiro said. He suspected that the two men would continue to work together, but the suspicion and anger would grow. And in the end, it would be bad for both of them, even if one did not kill the other.

Tilley pushed his plate away. "I can't eat any more of this slop."

Manjiro sawed off another bite of the meat.

The next day, they registered as gold miners and

decided to earn their stake by working in a mine. The wage was four dollars a day, to be paid at the end of the month.

By the end of the first week in the mine, Manjiro's palms had blistered, and the blisters had burst. His back ached and his legs hurt. But as time went on, his palms healed and toughened, and his back stopped hurting. He was now able to concentrate on conversations going on between others. He overheard discussions about the best ways to mine for gold.

One of the things he learned was that John Marshall, the man who discovered gold in California and started the rush, had found nuggets wherever he dug in gulches. With such mining, called placer mining, some men dug in or beside streams. Others scooped up rocks, sand, and gravel from beneath the water. They then "washed" the mixture in sheet iron pans to separate out the heavier gold. Sometimes there was dust, sometimes nuggets.

Manjiro and Tilley decided that when they quit the mine, they would dig as Marshall had, but not in gulches. They staked their claim four miles from the mining settlement and beyond isolated shacks, beside a stream. Water running down through gulches fed the stream. It was obvious that in times past the stream had run wider, over rocky earth that was now dry.

After three months of work in the mine, they had earned $180 each. It was enough to continue to pay for their lodging and food, to buy blankets for the

times they decided to stay out overnight, and to purchase shovels and pans.

"The contractor has cheated us, you know," Tilley
said. "I'm going to give him a farewell gift—a bloody
nose."

Between work on the lumber boat and working in the
mine, Tilley had become so strong he could make his
muscles jump. It concerned Manjiro that his friend
was so proud of his physical strength. "If you wish,"
he said. "But I prefer not to watch. I remember too
well what happened to the Irishman."

Tilley stopped flexing his biceps. "You do have a
way of cooling a man's temper," he said.

This capacity of the Americans to be their own worst
enemy, Manjiro thought, was something he would
never understand about them. In his years at sea, he
had more than once seen men nearly kill each other
over a trifle. "There is a better way to get our revenge,"
he said. "We will find much gold."

21
The Adventurer

On bad days, neither Manjiro nor Tilley found any gold. On good days, Manjiro might exchange his find for eight dollars in silver when they went back into town, and Tilley's might bring ten dollars. The next day, he might find more gold than Tilley did.

One day Manjiro found an exceptionally large nugget. *It is as big as a hen's egg,* he thought. Without telling Tilley or giving any indication that he had made a good find, he buried the nugget and put a rock on top of the spot. He trusted his friend completely, but Tilley would become excited, and he didn't know how to hide his excitement.

When dusk came and Tilley said, "Let's go," Manjiro said, "The weather is pleasant. I think I will stay here." At night, thieves with gold-hungry eyes watched everyone going into the town. More than one man who had left his claim with gold had lost it to thieves. Some men had also lost their lives.

Tilley searched his face, which Manjiro knew revealed nothing.

"It'll be cold out here before the night's over," Tilley said.

"I have the blanket. It will not be too uncomfortable. Why do you not stay with me?"

"No, thanks," Tilley said. "Miserable as that bed is, it's better than the ground. You'd better keep my blanket, too."

Manjiro folded Tilley's blanket to make a cushion between the top of his head and the rock that sat on his gold. He rolled himself into his own blanket. Gazing up at the stars, he said, "God of all, I beg you to watch over me this night and through my journey."

There was no moon; the stars were brilliant. His eyelids grew heavy, and the stars stirred a memory that had never surfaced before. He was seven years old, sitting outside with his father. In his musical voice, his father told him about the constellations, and about the great blinking star that guided the fishermen. His father's voice faded; the little boy couldn't hear him anymore.

His father had left him! He was gone. Manjiro couldn't find him, or his mother, or his house. He was cold and hungry, wandering around on a rock island.

His own outcry awakened him, and he lay with his heart racing in alarm. A bad dream, that was all, a dream brought on because he was alone, and chilled. Tilley was right; it became cold out here at night. Shivering, he made a two-blanket roll and scrunched down in it.

He slept lightly so that he would be aware if anyone approached, awakened at daybreak, dug up his nugget, and went into town and to the assayer's office. His nugget brought almost six hundred dollars in silver. He did not have to concern himself about the assayer's telling anyone. An assayer who talked would not live long.

Added to the profits from the sale of the whale oil, it was enough, Manjiro decided.

He found Tilley eating breakfast and joined him. When they had finished eating, but Tilley still lingered with a cup of coffee, Manjiro said, "I am leaving today for Honolulu. I wish you luck and a happy life, Tilley."

Tilley searched his face as he had last night, but

Manjiro explained no further. It was better this way. Tilley, who knew him well, would suspect he had made a good find, keep digging in the streambed, and perhaps have similar luck. Other men would not suspect that he had made a good find. If he had, they would reason, he surely would not leave; he would continue to look for more gold in the same place.

Tilley stood and hugged Manjiro to his chest. "Be careful, John."

Manjiro picked up his canvas bag and went outside to join a mule train going down the mountain. At last he was ready to try to bring his native country and his adopted country together. At last he could do something for the men of the sea who had done so much for him.

Manjiro was delayed in San Francisco, where pandemonium reigned because California had just been admitted to the union. While he waited, he wrote a letter to the Whitfields. He told them about his plans, and spoke of all they had done for him. "And never will forget," he wrote.

He was finally able to leave aboard the steamer *Elisha* on October 24, 1850. For the first time in his life, he paid the fare rather than working his passage. The ticket cost twenty-five dollars.

Eighteen days later, he was in Honolulu. During the

trip, he had come up with the name of the whaling boat he would buy to take his friends and him back to Japan. He would call it the *Adventurer*.

Epilogue

Fudenojo was elated that Manjiro was now ready to implement his plan to open a trading post on Okinawa, the main Loochoo island, then to go home. Goemon had married, and surely could not take a foreign wife on such a journey. He swayed one way, then the other. But finally, no doubt partially due to pressure from his big brother, he decided to abandon his wife and go. Toraemon simply said that Honolulu was his home, that he would not leave.

Chaplain Damon ran an article in *The Friend* asking

for donations of clothing and equipment, and the people of Oahu responded generously. Manjiro was so optimistic that he would safely get home that he purchased scissors, thread, buttons, a mirror, and pots and pans for his mother.

Captain Whitmore of the *Sarah Boyd*, a merchant ship en route to China, agreed to take the Adventurer and its three-man crew. The *Sarah Boyd* left Honolulu on January 9, 1851, sailed as close to Okinawa as its route allowed, and lowered the *Adventurer* into a stormy sea.

As the crew rowed through the night, wind, hail, and freezing rain reminded Manjiro of the night their fishing boat had been wrecked in the storm. So did Goemon's sobbing. It did no good to reassure him that this time they had a seaworthy boat and navigation instruments.

When the *Adventurer* landed on a rocky shore on Okinawa, Manjiro and his friends were treated with curiosity and even hospitality after a man who spoke Japanese came. Fudenojo, who had best retained his native tongue, carried on long conversations with the man.

But Japanese officials, who had been notified by the Okinawans, soon arrived on horseback, arrested Manjiro and his friends, and took them to Nagasaki to stand trial.

As Manjiro had anticipated, their captors were

intrigued with America. Over and over he answered their questions. He described life in the United States with words and drawings of Fairhaven, American trains, and citizens enjoying picnics and rowboating.

The president of the country, he told the officials, rode his horse in the company of just two friends. Since the shogun was always heavily guarded, this amazed Manjiro's interrogators. They were intrigued, and somewhat horrified, when he told them American mothers gave their babies cow's milk. They tittered when he said people in that faraway country enjoyed reading in the outhouse.

Manjiro didn't know it, but outside the prison walls, young scholars were secretly writing and circulating stories in which he was a hero.

He and Fudenojo and Goemon were tried eighteen times, but it was to Manjiro that most of the questions were directed. He became so weary of the trials, first in one city, then another, that he sometimes lost his temper with his questioners.

The three were finally freed, but the whale boat, the gifts Manjiro had brought for his mother, and his personal belongings were confiscated. He especially grieved about the loss of his book on navigation.

A boat trip to Shikoku, and more questions and forms in Kochi, that island's capital, further delayed reunion with their families. But at last Manjiro walked up the dirt road toward Nakanohama. His mother, relatives, and other villagers had received word of his arrival and met him on the road. At first Manjiro and his mother simply stood and looked at each other.

Then, according to custom, she asked his name. Before he could answer, she burst into tears.

Later that day, Manjiro went to the burial grounds to report his return to his father, and to apologize for not saying good-bye when he had left to go fishing ten years before.

Three days after he reached home, he was summoned to Kochi. By this time, he realized that he had become a folk hero. Even the samurai of Shikoku were pleased that one of their island's people had matched wits with the "snobs" of Honshu—and won. It nevertheless surprised Manjiro when the lord of Kochi gave him a low samurai rank.

Along with the rank came a family name, Nakahama, derived from the name of his village. Nakahama Manjiro (in Japan, the family name comes first) liked wearing the samurai robes. But to demonstrate his feelings about the swords, he carelessly tied their hilts together with towels.

Captivated with Kochi and its old castle and homes, he moved into a house there, and shared his knowledge of the world outside Japan. The people soon started calling him *sensei sama* ("honorable teacher").

He was content with his quiet life, but it was not to remain so. In July 1853, runners arrived with an urgent message bearing the crest of Tokugawa—the royal family whose members had ruled Japan for 265 years. Manjiro was needed in Edo (Tokyo) at once! So that he would appear worthy of such an honor, the lord of Kochi quickly raised Manjiro's rank, and he left for Edo.

Commodore Matthew Calbraith Perry had arrived at Uraga Bay on July 8 with his black ships—two armed steamships with two sailing vessels in tow. What Manjiro had tried to do—open supply posts—Perry was now demanding on behalf of the president of the United States. American ships in the Orient especially needed a port where they could get water and wood. Perry also demanded better treatment of shipwrecked sailors on all Japanese-controlled shores. If Japan didn't cooperate, he said, many more armed steamships would come. In other words, if peaceful threats didn't work, gunfire would. Perry presented documents and left.

Upon leaving, Perry had said he would return in six months for an answer. The shogunate turned for counsel to their statesmen, who included clear-thinking Egawa Torozemon. It was he who recommended that Manjiro be summoned to Edo to translate the American papers.

Knowing that his countrymen did not take well to threats, Manjiro softened Commodore Perry's written demands and threats.

It is not true, as has often been written, that Manjiro

was in an adjoining room and was consulted and allowed to translate when Perry returned in February 1854. Manjiro was still not trusted enough for that and was kept behind barred doors miles away from Kanagawa, where Perry had been stopped before he could reach Edo. (With both of Perry's visits, the Japanese were successful in keeping him away from the shoguns' capital.)

But this time, the Japanese did have a translator, a pitifully subservient "nameless" man who crawled on his knees and kept his eyes lowered. Fortunately Perry did not behave in a threatening manner on his second visit.

Trade began with the United States, and in 1855, the old Japanese Exclusion Edict was revoked. People from other countries could now come to Japan, and its people could go to other countries. Thus began the final days of the Tokugawa Shogunate.

Although he went back to Shikoku on occasion to see his mother, Manjiro continued to live in Edo. He first lived with his friend Torozemon. Torozemon chose Manjiro's wife—beautiful O Tetsu, the daughter of a samurai fencing master. Manjiro later admitted that he followed American custom and kissed O Tetsu before they were married.

He helped with shipbuilding and, when he was commanded to do so, translated Bowditch's *New American Practical Navigator* into Japanese. The project, which took three years, would have been a challenge for any scholar. Manjiro did many other noteworthy things, including helping with shipbuilding and teaching in the college that eventually became Imperial University.

But perhaps his greatest contribution was that by helping to open Japan, he played a significant role in ending the Japanese feudal system. It drew to a close with the downfall of the Tokugawa Shogunate in 1867.

In the summer of 1870, Manjiro was part of a Japanese-sponsored delegation to Europe and America. Unannounced, he walked up to the Whitfield home on Sconticut Neck. The evening with Captain and Mrs. Whitfield, and their son and two daughters, was a joyous occasion. He had written to them about his wife and children; now he shared family matters.

Manjiro died on November 12, 1898, at the age of seventy-one. Dr. Nakahama Toichiro later wrote a book, *Nakahama Manjiro den*, about his father—the son of a poor fisherman not even allowed a family name.